Note to Readers

Although the Harrington and Wakamutsu families are fictional, the events they find themselves in are real. As America pulled out of the Great Depression, rumblings of war were all around. Japan was conquering countries in Asia. Germany, led by Adolph Hitler, was taking over nation after nation in Europe.

Many people in the United States didn't want to be in another war. But as time passed, attitudes toward going to war changed. Prejudice against Japanese-Americans also increased. People vandalized their businesses and threatened their safety.

The good news was that more people had jobs. Because of this, school attendance went up. There weren't special programs for extremely bright students. Instead, those children "skipped" grades. Some students finished school as much as two years early.

RUMBLINGS
of
WAR

Norma Jean Lutz

PUBLISHING, INC.
Uhrichsville, Ohio

In memory of Elizabeth Morgan Mattson: A grand lady!
To know her was to love her.

© MCMXCVIII by Barbour Publishing, Inc.

ISBN 1-57748-511-4

Published by Barbour Publishing, Inc., P.O. Box 719, Uhrichsville, Ohio 44683
http://www.barbourbooks.com

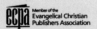

Member of the
Evangelical Christian
Publishers Association

Printed in the United States of America.

Cover illustration by Peter Pagano.
Inside illustrations by Adam Wallenta.

CHAPTER 1

Labor Day Picnic

"Pic-nic. Pic-nic. We're going on a picnic. It didn't rain. It didn't rain. We're going on a picnic."

Audrey slipped farther down beneath the covers in an attempt to drown out the silly song that her sister Barb was singing. The bouncy five-year-old woke up bright and cheery nearly every morning. Today, Labor Day, she was more excited than usual.

"Come on, Audrey. Get up. Help me tie my shoes." Barb was standing close enough to Audrey's bed to make it jiggle. The jiggling was irritating. Especially this early in the morning. Audrey lay still, pretending she was still asleep.

"Please, Audrey. I'm saying 'please.' You said 'please' is the magic word."

Barb now resorted to tugging on the bedcovers. "Go away," Audrey muttered. "Get Frank to tie your shoes. Or Isabel."

"They're all downstairs. You're the last sleepyhead. Please hurry. Eddie's been calling for me to come on."

Eddie was Barb's twin and constant companion. The two of them were like a couple of cub bears rollicking into mischief wherever they went. Both could be real pests at times. Especially when Audrey wanted to be left alone—which was now!

The bed bumped and creaked as Barb crawled up on it, placing both her feet close to Audrey's head. "Mama says if I walk downstairs with my shoes untied, I might fall."

Slowly Audrey uncovered her head. As she did, the aroma of perking coffee and frying bacon accosted her sleepy senses. Slowly she sat up and found herself nose-to-nose with the grinning face of her curly-haired little sister. "Hi," Barb said, giving a little wave.

"How can you be so noisy this early?" Audrey tried unsuccessfully to stifle a big yawn.

"It's not early. Please hurry and tie my shoes. Please?"

Pushing back the covers, Audrey swung her feet over the side of the bed. "If I tie them, will you leave me alone for a while?"

Barb nodded and her glossy dark curls bobbed. "Sure I will. I'm going to help pack the picnic basket. Mama said I could."

Audrey felt a twinge of guilt for lying in bed while the rest of the family joined in the preparations. Pulling Barb's foot into her lap, she tied first one little brown oxford and then the other.

A picnic at the park on Labor Day hadn't gotten her vote. Audrey was hoping they would go back to the Fairfax Hotel, where they used to live. Not that she'd voiced her opinion. What good would it do when everyone else was so gung ho on this picnic idea. She would have been terribly outnumbered.

6

"Your buttons are buttoned wrong." Audrey pointed to the front of Barb's playsuit.

Barb giggled as she looked down at her front. "They're all cockeyed, aren't they?"

"For sure. Here, let me fix them for you." Audrey unbuttoned and rebuttoned the playsuit. "You're all ready. Now scoot out of here and leave me alone."

Barb looked up at Audrey. "You'll hurry, won't you? You don't want to make us late for the picnic, do you?"

Audrey wanted to ask how a person could be late for a picnic, but she didn't. "We won't be late," Audrey assured her. "I promise."

With that, Barb threw her arms around Audrey's neck and planted a big wet kiss on her cheek. "Thank you, Audrey."

Audrey smiled in spite of her sour feelings. "You're welcome. Now get!"

Barb could be such a pain, but as soon as she was gone, their big bedroom suddenly took on a hollow, empty feeling. She got up and began to straighten the chenille bedspread. The spread was patterned with pink rosebuds and a trim pink border on a mint green background. She'd helped Mama pick out the colors for the room. The white bureau against the far wall was flanked by the vanity table with its large gold-frame mirror. A ruffled mint-colored skirt hung on the vanity and a matching tufted stool sat in front of it. Pink and mint green were repeated in the floral wallpaper and the priscilla curtains.

A person would have to be out of her mind to complain about such a lovely room. Yet, for some odd reason, Audrey still missed their old apartment at the Fairfax Hotel on Yesler Way. She knew it was silly, and she would never have admitted it to a soul, but she couldn't shake the feeling.

She reached down to pick up Barb's Shirley Temple doll

with her mop of lifelike curls. In a copy of Alice's *Silver Screen* magazine, she'd read about a Shirley Temple lookalike contest. Her older sister Alice was an accountant for a shipping firm and could afford to purchase a copy of the magazine every week.

If they ever decided to enter Barb in a Shirley Temple lookalike contest, she'd surely win, with her darling curls and pouty lower lip. All they'd have to do is bleach her curls to a blond color and she'd be a shoo-in.

Audrey lay the doll on Barb's bed and padded barefoot across the golden hardwood floor to the bureau. Pulling out a pair of clean shorts and a shirt, she held them up and studied them. Both were faded from so many washings, having been passed from Alice down to Isabel and from Isabel to Audrey. In the Harrington family, hand-me-downs were *real* hand-me-downs.

There on the closet door hung Barb's new dress all ready for her first day of kindergarten. Lucky Barb and Eddie had new clothes for school. Mama had told the rest of them that hand-me-downs would have to do. They'd spent a great deal of money on furniture for the new house, so cash for new school clothes was not available.

On the table between their beds sat Barb's school supplies: scissors, paste, a pencil box, a box of eight sharp new Crayolas, two Laddie pencils, and one Big Chief ruled tablet. Each day, several times a day, Barb counted each piece and rearranged the stack. The kindergartner was thrilled about her first day of school. Audrey felt just the opposite. Going to school at Queen Anne Grammar was going to be much different from Bailey Gatzert School on Yesler Way. She dreaded it. Jim Watson, Alice's boyfriend, called Queen Anne the snooty part of town. Since he was from Madrona Beach near Lake Washington, he should know. In high school, he'd played sports against teams from Queen Anne Hill.

Audrey dressed and then sat down at the dressing table to brush her hair. With the rat-tail comb, she straightened her center part. Two red barrettes were fastened into place, one on each side, letting the waves fall loosely to her shoulders. Mama would probably tell her she should have braided her hair for the day, but she didn't feel like wearing little-kid pig-tails today. Sharing a room with Barb made her feel enough like a baby. She didn't need pigtails to make it worse.

From the stairway, she could hear the voices coming up from the kitchen. They seemed so far away, as though every-one were in a faraway country. When they lived at the Fairfax, they were only a few steps away from one another. Mother once said they lived on top of one another. But that was what Audrey loved most about their apartment. That closeness, *plus* Mrs. Wakamutsu's wonderful Japanese cooking.

"Audrey!" Frank's voice called up the stairs. "Hey, slow-poke. The bacon's almost gone. You'd better hurry."

Bacon was Audrey's favorite part of breakfast. "You'd bet-ter save me a piece," she called back.

"Can't make guarantees for sleepyheads."

She grimaced at herself in the mirror. Her two-year-older brother could be so frustrating. "I'm coming," she called back.

Audrey still didn't hurry as she went down the stairs, through the living room, and into the kitchen at the back of the house. Every room in their new house was as big as a cave. The kitchen was no exception. In fact, it was the spacious, light-splashed kitchen that caused Audrey's mom to say yes to buying this house. One set of windows looked out over the dri-veway, and another set gave a view of their grassy backyard.

Over and over, Audrey had heard her mom say: "I want a kitchen big enough for all of us to sit down and eat together."

That was asking a lot for a family with seven children, but at long last Mama had her wish.

Nineteen-year-old Alice, looking lovely and poised as ever, stood at the sink washing pieces of chicken in preparation for frying them. Mother was cutting up the boiled potatoes for potato salad. Isabel had the silverware drawer open and was counting out the pieces to put into the wicker picnic basket.

"Well," Isabel said as Audrey came in, "it's about time. What a lazybones. You should be helping out." At fourteen, Isabel had begun to sound more like a mother than a sister.

"It's supposed to be a holiday," Audrey protested feebly. All this busyness made the guilt-pricks sharper than before.

Mother took one look at her and said, "Audrey, you should have braided your hair. It's a picnic."

"I want to wear it down." She filled her plate with the last of the bacon from the skillet on the stove, then took a bottle of milk from the fridge to fix a bowl of Wheaties.

Mama made them take turns getting their favorite cereal. Wheaties was Frank's favorite because it sported a picture of Jack Armstrong, the All-American boy. Frank never missed an episode of Jack Armstrong on the radio. He'd even sent off for the Jack Armstrong whistle ring, along with the secret whistle code. He and Kaneko and Abiko Wakamutsu used to play with their whistle rings together when they lived on Yesler Way. She hadn't seen the ring since they moved.

Pouring a glass of milk, Audrey stirred in heaping spoonfuls of Ovaltine to make the good-tasting chocolate-flavored drink. She, on the other hand, liked to listen to Little Orphan Annie's radio show. Orphan Annie loved to say:

> *For extra pep 'n' flavor keen,*
> *Drink chocolate-flavored Ovaltine!*

10

Spooning up the soggy Wheaties, she gazed out the windows to see Steve taking turns carrying the twins piggyback around the yard. Barb's squeals of laughter floated in through the open window. Audrey could remember when her older brother used to give her piggyback rides. She was too big for that sort of thing now. Sometimes she wished time could stand still. Change was such a scary thing—especially when so many changes came at once.

Yesterday, when they arrived home from church, Dad switched on the console radio in the living room in time to hear the news that Britain had declared war against Germany. Although Dad and Steve and Alice's boyfriend, Jim, talked on and on about the war, Audrey tried her best to ignore them. She didn't want to hear about the fighting and bombing and killing. In one direction, Japan was waging war on China, and in the other direction, Nazi Germany was attempting to take over Europe. When Audrey heard adults talking, they were asking, "Will the U.S. be next?"

The question that haunted Audrey was, if the U.S. went to war, would her beloved Steve have to go? She couldn't bear the thought. Steve was the only one in the family who loved books as much as she did. He seemed to understand when she preferred to have her nose buried in a good book rather than be doing her chores.

Now the twins were playing tag, and Steve was helping Dad clean out the trunk of their new burgundy-colored DeSoto. Long-legged and slender, Steve stood a few inches taller than Dad. With his dark hair and clear blue eyes, Audrey thought Steve was about the most handsome boy in the world. The twins kept running up behind him as though to scare him, and he joined in their fun, even as he was helping Dad. That was just like Steve.

11

Hurriedly Audrey finished the Wheaties, rinsed her dish and tumbler, and joined in the picnic preparations. Mother set her to cutting the carrot and celery sticks and wrapping them in squares of waxed paper.

Just as the golden-brown chicken was ready to be lifted from the skillets, Audrey heard Alice give a little gasp. Only one thing these days took Alice's breath away, and that was Jim Watson. Sure enough, in a moment they all heard the rattle of his old black Ford pulling into the drive. The thing shimmied and shook so that Audrey thought the fenders might fall off.

Alice dropped the towel in her hands and ran out the back door, letting the screen door slam just like Mama daily told all the rest of them not to do. Audrey guessed rules could be broken when you were grown up and had fallen in love.

"Mama!" Isabel cried out as she gaped out the window. "He's kissing her right in front of the whole world."

"Isabel Harrington, you get away from that window this minute," Mama ordered.

But Isabel ignored her. "Why should I miss out on what all the neighbors are seeing?" All dreamy-eyed, she added, "Mmm. It's so, *so* romantic. Almost like Rhett and Scarlett in *Gone With the Wind*." Turning from the window, she said, "Mama, do you think I'll ever have a man love me like Jim loves Alice?"

Just then, Frank popped in the back door and heard the question. Ruffling Isabel's hair, he said, "Love you, Dizzy-Izzy? You must be joking. Who'd wanna fall in love with a girl who can beat them at baseball, touch football, *and* marbles?"

Isabel shoved him away. "Oh, go away. Nobody asked for your feeble opinion."

Frank stumbled and acted like he was falling. "Ah, she got me. The tough woman got me. I'm dying. Argh! Gasp! Dying!"

Audrey laughed at their antics, but Mama said for them to stop it that instant. "Let's use our energy to get this food packed," she told them.

"Oh, yeah." Frank grinned sheepishly. "That's why I came in. Dad wants to know what's ready to be loaded."

Within the hour, both Jim's old Ford and the Harrington's DeSoto were loaded, and they were off to Kinnear Park. Audrey had even slipped in her newest Nancy Drew mystery without anyone noticing. With any luck, she'd have the whole thing read before the day was out.

Frank and Eddie chose to ride with Jim and Alice. That left more room in the back seat of the DeSoto. Dad was so proud of their car. He'd bought it from a fellow worker at the Boeing plant just a week or two earlier. He'd vacuumed it, washed and waxed it, and put on new tires.

But as with the new house, Audrey felt disoriented—as though she were riding along in someone else's body in someone else's place. Her place was in their old apartment at the Fairfax Hotel on Yesler Way. And Kaneko and Abiko were there waiting for her and Frank to come outside and play.

CHAPTER 2
The Golden Ring

The shady park wasn't far from their house, and Dad teased them about being softies—riding in the car when they could walk. But Mama said she'd like to see him walk and carry all the baskets of food, plus the blankets.

"Now, Lydia," he said, patting her arm, "we did it when we were kids."

Mama only smiled. Audrey figured Mama knew that Dad loved driving his new car and that he wasn't really protesting at all.

The park was crowded. They drove through the winding

shady drives looking for empty picnic tables. Finally Dad said, "Aw, who cares about tables? We'll spread the blankets under the shade trees." He motioned to Jim, who was following close behind, to park along the road, and they all piled out.

Audrey had to admit there was nothing as lovely as Kinnear Park down near the waterfront. The soft carpet of grass smelled sweet and clean as she spread a blanket over it. The food was quickly spread before them, and after Dad said grace over it, they dug in. The twins were finished eating and ready to play almost before the others had started eating. Steve said the two of them moved like greased lightning.

Since everyone was stuffed, they voted to wait until later in the afternoon to cut Mama's layered chocolate cake. Steve took the twins off for an adventurous walk on the path through the woods, and Frank and Isabel challenged Alice and Jim to a game of badminton. Steve never asked if Audrey wanted to come along on the walk, and the foursome never asked if she wanted to play. Nine, Audrey decided, was a nothing age to be.

As Audrey went to the car to retrieve her book, she heard Mama call out, "Don't overdo now, Frank. If you get winded, please stop right away."

Frank continued chasing around, knocking the feathered shuttlecock over the net as though she'd never said a word. Audrey knew it embarrassed Frank half to death when Mama called out to him like that.

Ever since Frank's last frightening coughing attack, Mama seemed to hover over him—more so even than with the twins. But then, Audrey, too, was terrified when Frank coughed and coughed and coughed and couldn't get his breath.

Taking her book, she walked a ways into the woods until she found a nice place to lean against a tree and read. Overhead the birds sang their hearts out, and in the distance the lonely ship whistles sounded in Elliott Bay.

She was nearly halfway through the book when she heard voices and footsteps along the path. Thinking it was Steve and the twins, she jumped up to hide behind the tree. What fun it'd be to scare the dickens out of them!

But it wasn't Steve and the twins. It was four girls who all looked to be about Audrey's age or a little older. Quickly she pulled her head back and pressed closer to the rough bark of the tree.

"And we can call our group the Golden Ring," one of the girls was saying.

"Oh, Grace," said another. "That's a wonderful name. How'd you ever think of it?"

"You know the answer to that, Marie. I'm smart, that's all."

All four of the girls giggled at the comment. As they passed by the tree, Audrey peered around at them. All four wore neatly cuffed shorts with blouses that matched. Their black-and-white saddle oxfords showed no scuffs on the white parts, and their anklets were neatly turned down.

"We'll be able to do most anything we want all during fourth grade," said the girl with long, honey-colored hair. She was the one named Grace. "Old deaf and blind Mrs. Brumley won't see a thing."

"Dumb-ly Mrs. Brumley," said another. The other three joined in the chant, singing, "Dumb-ly Mrs. Brumley," and then they burst into side-splitting giggles.

Audrey stared at the foursome as their voices faded into the distance. She glanced down at her faded play clothes and scuffed oxfords. Deaf and blind Mrs. Brumley? Now she dreaded the first day of school more than ever.

Just as Audrey suspected, Barb was up at the crack of dawn

the next morning, singing her little songs about going to school. *You would have thought it was Christmas or something,* Audrey thought as she turned over and tried to ignore the noise. It couldn't be anywhere near time to get up.

Lucky Alice. She got to go to work at Gaylor Shipping each day. None of this stuff about being the new kid at a new school, and all the worry that went with it, for her. Half-awake, Audrey dreamed of four girls surrounded by a glowing, halo-like golden ring. They walked along in a fuzzy cloud where saddle oxfords were never scuffed.

"Audrey! Audrey, are you awake?" It was Mama's voice from out in the hall.

"She's awake," Barb said with a giggle. "But she's acting like she's not."

"Everybody up," Mama said. "We don't want anyone to be late on the first day of school."

Audrey groaned. When she'd attended Bailey Gatzert, no one had had to tell her to get up. She loved going to school with all the kids in the neighborhood.

"Button me, please, Audrey." Jiggle, jiggle went the bed. "And tie my sash, too, please."

Audrey heaved a sigh and threw back the covers. This was silly. It should be the little sister who was frightened of going to school, not the big sister. Dutifully she buttoned the back of Barb's cute little print dress and tied the sash in a nifty bow, making sure the ends hung down just right.

"Thank you," Barb said primly. She picked up her armload of school supplies and went out the door. Audrey watched her, wondering what the girl would do for the next three-quarters of an hour before it was time to leave the house.

Standing in front of her closet, Audrey closed her eyes and grabbed a dress. It didn't really matter which one. She was thankful that Frank was still in grade school with her. Walking into the school with him would make things a little easier.

Mama asked the twins if they wanted her to come along on their first day. They said no. She was asking the wrong ones, Audrey thought as she pulled on her brown school shoes and tied the laces. She was the one who felt like holding Mama's hand today.

Steve took the bus to the high school. The junior high Isabel attended was in the opposite direction of Queen Anne Grammar. Audrey marveled that Isabel didn't seem a bit afraid. Frank was the same way. In fact, Frank had gone out looking for boys his age the very day they moved in. "If we'd come earlier in the summer, I'd have found a few," he said after a fruitless search.

Dad said they lived on the edges of the Queen Anne Hill community and there were mostly older folk in their immediate neighborhood. "You'll make friends at school," Dad had promised.

When they arrived at the playground, the first thing Audrey noticed was that everyone's face looked alike. At her old school, located smack in the middle of the international district, there were kids of all races and all nationalities. Dad called it the melting pot of the city. No one was really like anyone else, yet everyone was accepted. As the white faces stared at this new family coming into their world, Audrey wished she had taken time to appreciate her old school more when she was there.

Queen Anne Grammar was a buff brick building, rather new looking, long and low and spread out. It was nothing like stocky, two-story, old worn-out Bailey Gatzert. The chain-link fence here was sturdy and in good repair. The teeter-totters, jungle gym, swings, and slippery slide looked newer as well.

Silently the four Harrington children walked up the front

steps. The twins were a bit more subdued, and they moved closer to one another. How Audrey wished she had someone to hang close to all day.

Frank stepped ahead to open the front door, and they filed into the front hallway, which was lined with trophy cases. Filled-up trophy cases. Audrey wondered if this school had won every prize in every school event in the city.

Though they hadn't discussed it, Audrey thought Frank was going to go with her to take the twins to the kindergarten room. She was wrong. After they stopped in the office to learn where their rooms were located, Frank said, "You go on and take the twins to their room. I'll see you at lunch."

"I'm going home for lunch, remember?"

"I'll probably see you at recess then." And he was gone. The traitor.

Though most of the students were out on the playground, a few were in the hall, probably looking for their classrooms as well.

There were three wings to the school—A, B, and C, the lady in the office explained. Audrey took the twins down the long hallway of C wing to the very end. There the friendly kindergarten teacher, looking not much older than Alice, met them at the door.

"Hello, there," she said. "I'm Miss Appleton."

Eddie giggled. Leaning over to Barb, he said, "Do we bring apples to Miss Appleton?" Then Barb giggled.

"Some students do," said Miss Appleton. "You must be the Harrington twins."

Barb lifted up her armload of stuff. "I have all my supplies right here. I'm ready for school."

"I see you are ready," Miss Appleton answered. Then she smiled at Audrey as though they had a secret together. "Come in, children, and I'll show you where to put your things away."

The twins never looked back. The teacher glanced back at Audrey, mouthed "Thank you," and turned away as well.

Now Audrey had to walk all the way back down C wing by herself. The fourth-grade room was down A wing on the opposite side of the office.

As she approached the main hall again, a girl came running around the corner and nearly slammed right into her. Audrey would have recognized that flowing honey-colored hair anywhere. It was the girl she'd seen in the park.

After catching her balance, the girl said, "Hey, you need to watch out where you're going."

Audrey hadn't been the one who was running, but she said nothing. She just kept on walking.

When she found the fourth-grade room, she quickly discovered why the girls at the park said Dumb-ly Mrs. Brumley. Stepping inside, she saw an elderly woman standing at the blackboard, writing on the board with a shaky hand that was etched in wrinkles and blue veins. Her close-cropped thin gray hair allowed bits of pink scalp to show through. *Why did the school board allow such an old woman to continue teaching?* Audrey wondered.

She stood at the door a moment. No other students were in the room. Audrey hoped that meant she could choose where she wanted to sit. She cleared her throat in hopes of being noticed. The teacher didn't notice. Audrey stepped farther into the room, hoping her footsteps would attract attention. Nothing. Mrs. Brumley kept on writing. She wrote a Scripture verse, then added the date, September 5, 1939, and her name, Mrs. Iola Brumley.

Clearing her throat again, Audrey took two more steps and said, "Excuse me, please."

"What?" Mrs. Brumley turned about. "Well, well. A new student. You aren't supposed to be in here yet. All the children are out on the playground."

Didn't this teacher even want to know who she was? "May I put my things down?"

Audrey's arms were getting tired of holding the books and supplies.

Mrs. Brumley waved a veined hand, covered lightly with chalk dust. "Put them anywhere and get on out to the playground, child."

"Yes, ma'am." Audrey didn't hurry as she walked around the room looking for an empty desk. She found one midway in the row nearest the windows. Setting her things down, she walked slowly to the main hall and out the front door. Just as she opened the door, a loud electric buzzer sounded, and she nearly jumped out of her skin.

"Get in line," came a voice from behind her.

The students were lining up by grades, but Audrey had no idea which grade was which until she saw the girl with the honey-colored hair. She went to the end of that line.

As she walked with the others up the stairs and down the hall, she noticed a girl in line ahead of her who was nearly as tall as a sixth grader. Not just tall, but big-boned. And when she walked, she limped along with a strange rolling gait. The special-built shoes, one with a sole thicker than the other, were uglier than Audrey's brown oxfords. Much uglier. The girl's hair looked like it hadn't seen a comb in days. Audrey tried not to stare.

After Mrs. Brumley brought her class to order, which took a little while, she called the roll. That's when Audrey learned that the girl with the limp was Hulda Goddard. And the girl with the pretty honey-colored hair was Grace Farmington.

21

When Audrey's name was called, she answered so softly, Mrs. Brumley didn't hear. Looking up, she scanned the room, glaring over her small reading glasses as though she had two sets of eyes. "Audrey Harrington?" she said, raising her voice. "Speak loudly and clearly please."

Some of the kids snickered.

Blushing, Audrey answered in a louder voice. "Here." They snickered again.

After the morning Scripture reading, prayer, flag salute, and singing of the national anthem, Mrs. Brumley reviewed who had which textbooks and workbooks and which ones still needed to be ordered. When those details were out of the way, she asked the students to take out their math books.

By this time, Audrey had the four girls from the Golden Ring figured out. Grace, of course, and a dark-haired girl named Marie Sikes. The other two were Yvette Reid and Claire Mayer. The four were sitting in a close little group just over from Audrey. After they made a joke, the girls would hook little fingers, like a secret handshake. Audrey saw no other girls hooking little fingers except the four in the Golden Ring.

They whispered during class time, but Mrs. Brumley didn't seem to mind. Or perhaps she couldn't hear.

"How many of you know your multiplication tables by heart?" Mrs. Brumley asked. "All the way up to twelve."

Audrey raised her hand without thinking. She should have waited a moment. Hers was the only hand up. Unless there was one behind her. . . .

"Only one student?" Mrs. Brumley asked. Her tone was one of shock.

Audrey put her hand down quickly, feeling the cold stares around her. The four in the Golden Ring were twittering softly.

Was there something wrong with knowing all the times tables by heart?

Alice had helped her with fractions and decimals last winter, but when Mrs. Brumley asked who knew about fractions and decimals, Audrey wouldn't have raised her hand for anything.

The morning dragged on until it was time for recess. At least Audrey thought it was supposed to be recess. Instead, they were to report to the gymnasium for a physical education class, as Mrs. Brumley called it. Students in junior high schools and high schools had phys ed classes, but a grammar school? This didn't sound like much fun to Audrey.

The phys ed teacher's name was Miss Browne. Miss Browne carried an important-looking clipboard and had a big voice that filled the entire gymnasium. The booming voice bounced against the high ceilings and came down on their heads like a driving rain. Dressed in navy blue shorts, a white blouse, and trim white sneakers, Miss Browne shouted, "All right, everybody. File in and sit on the floor in neat, straight rows."

Hulda Goddard's special shoes make an awful clomping sound as she made her roll-step right up to the front, right under Miss Browne's nose.

"Wouldn't you know? It's tottery, doddery Goddard," hissed a voice down the row from Audrey. Snickers followed. It was Grace and her adoring followers.

"Quiet!" came Miss Browne's booming voice. "I'll be the only one talking in this room."

Grace whispered, "You call that talking?" Again the girls snickered.

Amazing how good they were at snickering. Audrey wondered if they did anything else. She was already beginning to dislike Queen Anne Grammar—most intensely.

When Miss Browne described the year's plan for phys ed class—the gym suits they had to wear, showers they had to take, laps they had to run, and sports they all must be involved in—Audrey was ready to go back to Yesler Way and live with the Wakamutsus!

CHAPTER 3
Library Day

The dramatic theme music for the *Romance of Helen Trent* was playing on the radio when Audrey and the twins walked into the kitchen for lunch. After Helen Trent would come *Our Gal Sunday.* All through the summer as she helped Mama around the house, Audrey listened to the soap operas to see what would happen the next day. It was a make-believe world where the problems were many, but there were always answers.

Her favorite was *Just Plain Bill,* "a story about people who might be your own next-door neighbor," the announcer told listeners. But Audrey couldn't think of anyone she knew who were like the people on the radio shows.

"To get your teeth doubly clean," the radio announcer was saying as Audrey washed up at the kitchen sink, "use Dr. Lyons' Tooth Powder. Dr. Lyons removes film and surface stain with its remarkable cleaning power."

Steve said once that if they believed everything the radio advertisers said, they'd have to use fifteen different tooth powders and twenty different kinds of laundry soap.

The wringer washer was sitting in the middle of the kitchen chugging away, giving off the clean soapy aromas of wash day. Audrey would have been more than happy to stay home and help hang the laundry out on the clothesline. Mama turned off the washing machine long enough to serve up their bowls of tomato soup and cheese sandwiches, then turned back to guiding the clothes carefully through the wringer into the rinse water.

Between doing the laundry and listening to the twins raving about their wonderful first day of kindergarten, Mama hardly had a moment to look at Audrey. How Audrey wished Mama would ask her how the day was for her. But even if she had, Audrey wasn't sure she'd be able to answer. After all, she didn't want to be a whiny baby. That's what Frank called her when she complained.

She did tell her mother about needing a gym suit. Mama looked up from the steamy laundry and pushed a lock of hair out of her face. "Really? I don't remember seeing that on the list."

"Whether it was or not, I still need it. We have physical education class every morning."

Mama just nodded. "I suppose I can run downtown after the wash is hung out and the twins finish their naps." And she went back to her work. *Ma Perkins* was coming on just as Audrey left to go back to school.

The afternoon was worse than the morning, only without Miss Browne's shouting. During geography, Audrey forgot for a moment where she was, and when Mrs. Brumley asked a question, her hand shot up before she could stop it.

"Show-off," she heard someone whisper. Unlike Miss Browne in the noisy gymnasium, Mrs. Brumley heard none of the whispering.

The afternoon hours dragged slowly by. At recess Audrey kept to herself, which was more than easy since no one paid a bit of attention to her. She didn't know which was worse, being ignored or being tormented like Hulda. Neither she nor Hulda seemed to fit in anywhere. The only difference was, Hulda fought back. For Audrey, it was safer to retreat.

Frank, on the other hand, was involved in a rousing, noisy game of baseball with all the other fellows. He was an outfielder, but at least he was in the game. Maybe it was easier being a boy. Tomorrow she'd bring a book to read at recess time.

"It's your week to do the ironing," Isabel said to Audrey as they set the table for supper that evening.

"I know, I know." Audrey certainly didn't need Isabel to tell her what jobs belonged to whom since Mama kept the job schedule posted on the corkboard beside the fridge. Anyone with eyes could see it. Actually it was Alice *and* Audrey's week. One week Mama and Isabel took on the bushel basket of ironing, the next week Alice and Audrey took it. But Isabel hadn't mentioned Alice.

The familiar chug of Jim's Ford sounded outside as he brought Alice home from work. He worked as a longshoreman for Gaylor Shipping.

"Will Jim be staying for supper?" Audrey asked, wondering if they needed another place setting.

"Well, we can't know that until Alice comes in, now can we?" Isabel snapped.

"I just asked," Audrey said softly. What had she done to make her older sister so snippity?

When a smiling Alice came through the door and they heard the sound of the Ford backing out of the drive, Isabel said to Audrey, "There's your answer." Audrey ignored her.

Alice was glowing, as she always was after she'd been with Jim for any length of time. "Hi, everyone," she said as she breezed through the kitchen. "I'll get changed and be right down to help."

Audrey watched her older sister with eyes of envy. She tried, without much success, to imagine what it would be like to belong to someone special like Alice belonged to her Jim.

Steve would be arriving shortly from his after-school job of pumping gas at the Tydol filling station. He always came home with grease up to his elbows and grimy fingernails. Audrey never thought he really liked doing such a messy job. But as he said, "It's a job."

Dad, on the other hand, wouldn't be there for supper. Since Dad had been working overtime at Boeing, Mama kept his supper warm in the oven.

All through supper the conversation danced about from one young Harrington to the next, as they told the happenings of their first day of school. Audrey said very little. Presently Steve happened to look over at her.

"You're awful quiet tonight, little sis." He stretched his long leg under the table and tapped her ankle with his foot. "Everything okay?"

She nodded. "Everything's okay," she replied, forcing her face to smile.

"I know what Audrey's problem is," Frank put in.

Audrey held her breath, hoping he wouldn't tell how she was off by herself at recess.

"What is it, Frank?" Barb asked, her face screwed up in a frown. "What's Audrey's problem?"

"Her class hasn't had library day yet. Ours is tomorrow."

"Library day?" Audrey was sure she hadn't heard Mrs. Brumley say anything about a library day.

Alice laughed. "Well, we all know everything's all right in Audrey's world once she locates the library."

"Hey, now," Steve countered. "Nothing wrong with loving a good book. Right, Audrey?"

"Right, Steve." It felt good to hear Steve talk as though the two of them had a special secret. But the feeling was fleeting as the conversation sailed right on. Well, at least she knew there was going to be a library day at Queen Anne School. Things were looking up—even if just a smidgen.

The girls in the Golden Ring chose the time in the locker room to gang up on Hulda. The more they made fun of her, the louder Hulda talked back to them. The louder she talked back in her raspy voice, the more they laughed at her.

"Move your stuff, Clubfoot," one of the Golden Ring said to her, pushing her clothes off the bench and onto the damp floor.

"You better cut that out right now," Hulda answered in her thick voice. "And I mean it, too."

"You better cut that out right now," another girl mocked.

Audrey wished someone would make them be quiet. But she knew she wasn't the one to do it. Secretly, she was glad it was Hulda and not her they were picking on. Yet even that thought ate at her midsection.

In gym class, the barking Miss Browne made them run laps around the gymnasium, and Hulda had to run right along with all the rest. Of course, she couldn't keep up in her clumsy rolling gait. Some of the faster runners passed her several times. Audrey had to give the girl credit. In spite of the rude remarks, Hulda kept on huffing and puffing around the gym.

Audrey learned that Friday was library day for the fourth graders. She could hardly wait. Friday was a welcome day anyway since it meant she'd have two whole days in a row away from Queen Anne School, but now it also meant she'd have fresh new books to read.

The library was located down the stairs just beneath the front office. It was more beautiful than Audrey could ever have imagined. Large, roomy, well lighted, and best of all, well stocked. Afternoon sunshine streamed in through the high windows, laying golden patches on the glossy hardwood floor.

"May I have your attention, fourth graders," came a high melodic voice. The murmuring and whispering stopped as a petite brown-eyed young lady stepped into the center of their group.

"My name is Miss LaVolette, and I'm your new librarian. Welcome to your library day." She went over the rules of checking books out for only one week and warned them to return books and not lose them. "If you lose a library book, we may have to suspend your borrowing privileges."

"Say," whispered a boy standing directly behind Audrey. "What a great reason to lose a book. I don't want to borrow any anyway. I hate reading."

Hate reading? Audrey couldn't imagine such a thing. As the pretty librarian continued to talk, Audrey began to scan the shelves nearest her. There were books of fantasy, adventure, mystery, and plenty of biographies of famous people. As soon as Miss LaVolette stopped talking, Audrey grabbed a couple books and went to the reading area off in the corner. They had a full hour of library time.

With about fifteen minutes left, Audrey chose five books from the shelves and stood in line to check them out. When she stepped up to Miss LaVolette's desk, the librarian looked up at Audrey, her soft brown eyes wide. "Five books?"

Audrey nodded, feeling her face grow red. "Is that all right?"

"There's a limit of two per week. I mentioned it when I was explaining the rules a moment ago."

That must have been the moment when Audrey stopped listening and started studying book titles. "I'm sorry. I must have missed that part. But I'll have two books read by Monday."

Miss LaVolette chuckled. "I guess you like to read."

Audrey nodded. She wished she could tell this sweet lady just how much she loved books, but there were too many ears nearby.

"Chose two for this time," Miss LaVolette directed. "If you continue to bring your books back on time, we'll let you check out more."

Reluctantly Audrey chose two out of the five and turned to place the other three back on the shelves. As she did, she saw the girls in the Golden Ring hovering near the end of the line of fourth graders. They were one row away from where Audrey had to return one of the biographies.

Grace's loud singsong whisper came floating over the bookshelf, "Oh please, Miss LaVolette. Please let me check out fifty books. I promise I'll have them all back by next week."

"Oh you silly, silly girl," answered another mocking voice, "just take the whole library home with you. Why, we don't mind at all."

Snickers and giggles followed as though that were the funniest joke of the century. Her face burning, Audrey slipped the books back into their places and hurried out the door and back to the classroom. Those girls were probably hooking little fingers as they laughed.

As if things couldn't get any worse, later that afternoon, Mrs. Brumley handed back their spelling tests. Laying Audrey's paper on her desk, the teacher announced to the whole world, "First spelling test of the year, and Audrey Harrington received the only perfect score in the entire class. Fine job, Audrey. Fine job!" And the old lady actually patted Audrey's shoulder with her thin vein-lined hand.

Audrey shuddered inwardly and wanted to drop through the floor. Sure enough, when school was dismissed and the students filled the halls, she heard the mocking voices behind her, "Fine job, Audrey Einstein. Fine, fine job. We're so, *so* proud of you."

Audrey was sure she was going to die right there in the front hall of Queen Anne School!

CHAPTER 4

Miphibosheth

On Saturday night, Alice had a date with Jim, and Steve was working at the filling station. But the rest of the family planned to spend the evening with the Wakamutsus. Audrey was pleased. A hurricane could be blowing Seattle off the map, yet inside the Wakamutsu home it would still be serene and peaceful. Mr. and Mrs. Wakamutsu simply wouldn't allow it to be any other way.

The Wakamutsu children had been their playmates all the years the Harringtons had lived at the Fairfax. Kaneko and Abiko not only played games with Frank, but they always included Audrey as well. And even though their older sister,

Yoshiko, was Isabel's age, she never treated Audrey like a little kid. In fact, Audrey had never known a left-out feeling while she lived there.

Even Isabel seemed happy that they were going back for a visit. As they drove through downtown Seattle in the DeSoto, Isabel wondered aloud if Yoshiko would still be her friend.

Mother tried to calm her fears. "Don't worry, Isabel," she said, "you know how loyal the Japanese are. Yoshiko will never stop being your friend."

Dad parked on the street in front of the large red-brick building. The sidewalk was flanked by almost every business imaginable. A friendly Italian restaurant stood next to the stairs that led to the front entrance of the hotel. On down the street was the second-hand store where Mama and Dad purchased many of their clothes when they first arrived in Seattle. Next came the barber shop, and on the corner was the cigar shop.

Down the other way was the union office with the filthy fly-specked front windows, the Chinese laundry, and the burlesque house, where they were forbidden to even peek inside one of the painted windows. Audrey marveled that everything was just as they'd left it. Even the heavy aromas from the Italian restaurant were exactly the same.

As soon as Mrs. Wakamutsu politely answered the door and ushered them in, Audrey could smell the aroma of rice balls with pickled plums in the center. Her favorite. She was the only one of the Harringtons who loved the bright red salty plums as much as the Wakamutsus.

Bowing and offering polite greetings, Mr. and Mrs. Wakamutsu led the Harringtons into the dining room, where they took their seats. The small dining room was adjacent to Mrs. Wakamutsu's kitchen. Everything in the hotel was compact and orderly.

Mother had brought along two freshly baked pies, which Mrs. Wakamutsu insisted she shouldn't have done. But she graciously took them and set them on the kitchen counter. Mama had always said she hoped the Wakamutsus' good manners would rub off on all her children.

As they ate, Dad and Mr. Wakamutsu talked about the rumors of war with Japan. "It is as though the madness of Hitler has touched the militarists of Japan," said Mr. Wakamutsu, shaking his head gravely. "And whatever madness they perform, those around here blame us."

Frank lay down his red-lacquered chopsticks. "No one can blame you for what's happening clear across the Pacific, can they? Why, that would be like blaming every German-American for what Hitler is doing."

"They can," said Mr. Wakamutsu, "and they do." He paused while his wife brought a fresh pot of tea to the table. "If there is war between Japan and this country, my wife and I will be considered enemy aliens."

Audrey nearly choked on her pickled plum. "But Mr. Wakamutsu, it's not your fault that you're not a citizen," she protested. "The law won't let you. Isn't that right?"

Mr. Wakamutsu gave a polite nod in her direction. "Quite so, Audrey. We are prevented from becoming citizens by the Immigration Law passed way back in 1924. Perhaps because people are afraid of us. I do not know."

Audrey couldn't imagine anyone being afraid of this kind and gentle man.

"What's an alien?" Eddie wanted to know.

Ignoring his little brother, Frank said, "You want to become citizens and can't, and yet you're considered aliens because you're not citizens. Doesn't make much sense to me."

"Thank goodness *we're* all citizens," Kaneko said, waving

35

his hand to include himself, his brother, and his sister.

"That's right," Abiko echoed. "I'm no alien."

"What's an alien?" Eddie asked again.

"Someone who's not a citizen of a country," Mother answered him.

"What's a citizen?" Barb asked.

Dad chuckled. "Five years old—the question-asking age." Turning to the twins, he said, "I'll explain it when we get home tonight."

"Enough of all this depressing talk," Yoshiko said. "Mama-san, may we be excused so I can show our guests the new addition to the family?"

"What new addition?" Frank asked.

"You'll see," Yoshiko said, her almond eyes squinting as she smiled.

"What?" Dad teased her. "No apple pie?"

"We can have pie later," Abiko said as he scooted back his chair. "May we go, Mama-san?"

"You may," Mrs. Wakamutsu said in her quiet voice.

As they filed out into the apartment hallway, Frank said, "What do you mean about a new addition? You have new people coming into the hotel almost every day."

"Not a tenant, silly," Kaneko said, punching Frank in the shoulder.

"To my room," Yoshiko ordered.

"Wait for me," Barb called as she brought up the rear. Audrey waited for her, then picked up her little sister in her arms.

They followed after Yoshiko, trying to keep their giggles down so as not to disturb other guests.

Yoshiko opened the door to her cozy little bedroom, lined with bookshelves full of books and exquisite handmade

Japanese dolls in silk kimonos. There, lying in the center of her bed, was a half-grown gray and white kitten.

"Oh-h," Barb breathed. "A kitty-cat."

"I thought your mama said she wouldn't allow you to have pets," Isabel said as she sat down beside the kitten and began petting it.

Yoshiko laughed. "We kept pestering her, and she finally gave in. Right, boys?"

"Right," Abiko said with a big smile. "And Mittens has already earned her keep. She killed two mice in one week."

"And that convinced Father right away to let us keep her," Yoshiko said. "She was a stray out in the alley, and we fed her for a while before asking if we could keep her."

Abiko crawled over the foot of the bed and sat down in the corner. "Mama said that if her grandfather were alive and were here, he'd call the cat a goblin."

"A goblin?" Isabel said, petting the kitten. "How could anyone call this cute little thing a goblin?"

Audrey pushed in and sat Barb down on the bed so they could pet the kitten, too. Its fur was silky and felt soft and clean. "She doesn't look like an alley cat," Audrey said, feeling the rumbling of purring beneath her fingertips.

"You can bet Yoshiko has already given her a couple baths," Abiko said.

"She may hate water," Yoshiko said, "but it's easier to get her into the tub than either of my two brothers."

Her joke set them all to laughing. The fun and laughter made Audrey forget for a moment that she didn't live in their comfortable old apartment where she fit in. Even Isabel seemed to be her old self and not so bossy.

After fussing over Mittens, they all went to the vacant lot to play kickball until it grew too dark to see the ball. Kickball in the vacant lot with the Wakamutsu children was much different than kickball in phys ed class at Queen Anne School. Even Barb and Eddie joined in. Kaneko and Abiko were especially careful to kick the ball gently to the little ones.

Later, they went back in, laughing and hot and dusty and sweaty. Mrs. Wakamutsu let them take their pie and glasses of milk into the boys' bedroom, where they turned on the radio and listened to *Inner Sanctum* and *The Shadow.* The grownups were listening to *The Hit Parade,* which was pretty boring.

Audrey had to move over a stack of comic books to make room to sit on the floor. The Wakamutsu boys and Frank used to have contests to see who could collect the most *Captain Marvel* comics. The Wakamutsus usually won. They had twice the allowance money as Frank.

The radio shows were spooky, and the boys wanted to turn out the lights and listen in the dark. And they did—until Barb started crying. Yoshiko quickly took Barb onto her lap, wiping away her tears and telling her everything was all right. Audrey thought that Eddie looked just as scared, but he didn't cry.

After that, they left the lights on, but they still had a good time. And because it was such a special night, they were each allowed to have two pieces of pie. Barb couldn't eat all hers, so the boys finished it off for her.

As they drove through brightly lit downtown Seattle back to Queen Anne Hill, Barb was sound asleep, leaning heavily against Audrey's side. How Audrey wished the evening could have lasted forever.

When they stopped at the house, Dad came around to the back seat and gently lifted Barb up in his arms to carry her inside. As he did, she roused enough to ask in a sleepy voice, "Daddy, what's an alien?" making all the rest of them laugh. Eddie, however, was still wide awake.

Later, Audrey lay awake, thinking about the fun she'd had that evening. Suddenly she heard Alice coming in from her date. Through the walls, she could hear Alice and Isabel's excited voices chattering together. Audrey bet Alice was telling Isabel all about her date, the places where she and Jim had gone and the romantic things they'd done together.

She heard Alice turn on the phonograph and put on the Glen Miller recording of "Somewhere Over the Rainbow." Alice had lots of phonograph records, and lucky Isabel got to share them now that they were in the same bedroom.

When they'd lived at the Fairfax, Audrey and Barb slept in the upper bunks of the two bunk beds, and the older girls were below. Audrey would lay there pretending to be asleep, yet listening to the older girls' conversations. Now she was stuck off with the baby as though she, too, were a baby in the family. And they didn't have a phonograph player in their room.

Why couldn't Isabel have shared a room with Barb, and let Audrey be with Alice? No one had even asked her opinion in the matter. Perhaps her opinions didn't even count.

Thick foggy mist hung in the air as they left for church the next morning. Jim had come by early to pick up Alice. They sang in the choir, and extra rehearsals were held before Sunday school started. Alice came home so late and rose so early. Audrey wondered how her sister could go on so little sleep.

The big stone church with its heavy bell tower was situated at the edge of the downtown business district. Dad had promised them when they moved that they would continue attending their old church, for which Audrey was thankful. A few of the girls she'd gone to school with at Bailey Gatzert were in her Sunday school class. Everything had been fine during the summer. But now that school had started, her friends Jane Ann and Lisa were talking about activities at school, and none of it concerned Audrey.

When they asked about Queen Anne School, all she could say was, "It's okay." Which, of course, it was not. Not even close.

Audrey loved Pastor Colston. He was young and had a young attractive wife and two cute little sons. His sermons were colorful and easy to understand. She hardly ever fidgeted when he preached. Which is more than she could say for Eddie and Frank. They were always getting into trouble. Mama said Frank was a bad influence on Eddie. Audrey agreed.

"Frank, you should be setting a good example," Mama would say in her exasperated tone.

"I'm trying," Frank would answer in a feeble attempt to defend himself.

"You're not trying hard enough," Mama would reply.

It was a conversation that everyone in the family knew by heart.

This morning, Pastor Colston was preaching from the Book of 2 Samuel, using the story of Jonathan's crippled son who had the long name of Miphibosheth. King David had made an oath to show kindness to the family of his friend Jonathan, Pastor explained. After Jonathan had died and David became king, he remembered his promise and began to search the land for members of Jonathan's family.

Audrey turned to the passages in her small white Bible. She followed along, listening to Pastor tell how David looked for Miphibosheth. When he found the man, he brought him into the king's own house. But Miphibosheth was crippled in his feet.

"Poor, Miphibosheth," Pastor said. "He was embarrassed and ashamed. He bowed down and said, 'What is thy servant, that thou should look upon such a dead dog as I am?' " Pastor Colston smiled. "What a surprise was in store for this man who was lame and unable to walk normally. He was told that he would eat bread at the king's table every day."

Audrey thought about Hulda being lame in her feet and the strange way she walked. She was sort of like Miphibosheth, although Audrey couldn't imagine brash Hulda bowing down and saying she was like a dead dog.

"King David," Pastor continued, "sent for one of Saul's servants and commanded him and his sons and servants to till the land and bring the fruit of it to Miphibosheth." Closing his Bible, Pastor looked over the congregation and said, "God is faithful to His promises, even more so than King David. He doesn't care if we are lame or crippled. He loves us and wants us all to come and eat at His table."

As they stood to sing "Come and dine, the master calleth, come and dine," Audrey wondered if Hulda knew that God loved her in spite of her crippled feet.

CHAPTER 5
Alice's Surprise

At school on Monday morning, Audrey met Miss LaVolette in the hallway. The librarian was dressed in a pale yellow dress with a knife-pleated skirt and softly bloused bodice. Her short, curly hair was fluffed perfectly around her tiny face, and her red lipstick was flawless.

"Good morning, Audrey," she said. As Audrey drew near, she caught a whiff of Evening in Paris cologne. Alice used that.

Audrey was surprised that the librarian had remembered her name. She mumbled her greeting and started to pass by, but Miss LaVolette stopped, so Audrey stopped as well.

"Did you finish your two books over the weekend?"

Audrey nodded, hoping no one was listening. She'd finished the books all right, but Isabel had called her a lazybones and accused her of using reading as an excuse to get out of work.

"Tell you what," Miss LaVolette said. "Since you're such a book lover, if you get here a little bit early in the morning, come down to the library and I'll let you switch out your two books for two more."

Audrey felt her heart skip a beat. "Honest? Could I do that?" She was wondering if she could force herself to get up earlier in the morning.

"You may do that," Miss LaVolette answered, her brown eyes smiling.

"Thank you very much," Audrey breathed, then hurried on to put her books away.

Later, as they were filing into the classroom, one of the girls in the Golden Ring was mimicking Hulda's strange way of walking. It made everyone else laugh. Mrs. Brumley's back was turned, and she didn't seem to know anything was happening.

"Dummies." Hulda dropped heavily into her seat, making her desk shake—and the one in front of her as well. "Bunch of dummies is all you are," she said in a grating whisper. Her words made them laugh all the more. Grace and Marie hooked little fingers across the aisle.

Audrey realized they wanted Hulda to say something. And she always did.

All the girls had purchased their gym suits, and showers after phys ed class were required. Most of them turned on the water in the stalls, then jumped in quickly and back out just as quickly. Not Hulda. She was the only one who stood inside the curtained stall for any length of time and actually used the soap.

One day after gym class was over, the hot, sweaty girls crowded into the locker room laughing and talking. When

43

they'd done their usual spritz in and out of the showers, Audrey heard Marie Sikes say, "Hey, Grace. Look here." Audrey turned to see that she was pointing to Hulda's clothes lying in a rumpled pile along with the unsightly built-up shoes.

"Well, well," Grace said, running her hairbrush through her long, silky hair. "What do you know. Dirty laundry."

The other girls giggled. Hulda's dresses were plain and unattractive, and her one red cardigan sweater, which she wore nearly every day, was frayed in the cuffs of the sleeves.

"What do we do with dirty laundry?" Grace asked, laying her brush down on the edge of the sink.

"Why, we wash them, of course." This bit of wisdom came from Yvette Reid. Audrey thought petite Yvette looked much too innocent to be part of the Ring, but who could tell. Yvette picked up the clothes with one hand while holding her nose with the other. "Shall I?"

"Dirty laundry needs washing," Marie said with a smirk. "We're doing her a favor."

Yvette dumped the clothes into a shower stall, and Marie tossed the shoes and stockings in after them.

Audrey quickly pulled on her skirt and blouse, acting as though she heard nothing. Inside she wanted to scream at them to stop. Her shoes and stockings were on in a flash, and she was going out the door of the locker room when she heard Hulda hollering because her clothes were nowhere to be found.

How Audrey wished she could do something. But what? Her stomach was churning as she hurried back to class. Later, when class took up, Hulda was missing. Audrey learned later that the girls told Miss Browne that Hulda took a shower with her clothes on.

Would Miss Browne have believed such a story? Maybe so. After all, everyone said Hulda was not right in her head.

44

Grace and Marie said she was madder than a March hare. Audrey wasn't so sure about that. Just because her feet were crippled didn't mean her brain was.

Poor Hulda was driven home by Miss Browne and didn't come back to school that day.

Audrey had no trouble getting up the next morning. She was up and dressed before Mr. Stokley, the milkman, pulled up to the house to deliver their daily milk and cream. When it was time to leave for school, Frank and the twins weren't at the front door waiting for her. She was there first.

When Frank asked why she was ready so early, she told him about Miss LaVolette's offer to let her come to the library before school.

"I like Miss LaVolette," Barb said as she skipped along beside them.

"Me, too," Eddie echoed. "She's nice. She comes to our room and reads us a story for story time. I sit on the blue circle at story time."

"I sit on the yellow circle. Yellow's my mostest favorite color. Sunshine is yellow."

As the twins walked ahead of them, Frank said, "You must've made an impression on the librarian. What did you do?"

Audrey smiled. "Actually, it's because I wasn't listening. I didn't hear her say we could only check out two books, and I had five. Had to put three of them back."

Frank laughed. "I guess only a librarian could appreciate that."

As they talked about school, Audrey considered telling him about the incident with Hulda in gym class. How they had soaked her clothes. But before she had a chance to decide, two boys from down the street called to him.

"See you later," Frank said, and sprinted off. Audrey wished someone were calling to her to hurry and join them.

Before going downstairs to the library, Audrey glanced about to see if anyone was watching. But it was early and the halls were nearly empty, so she felt safe.

Miss LaVolette was smiling when Audrey came in. "Good morning, Audrey," she said, peering over a low bookshelf. "How's my fourth-grade avid reader?"

"Fine, thank you." Audrey glowed under the warm compliment. "Shall I lay these here?" She put her two books on the librarian's desk.

"Yes, please. I'll check them in later. Come here. I want to show you something."

Audrey followed her into a small room behind the check-out desk. Waving to a counter, Miss LaVolette said, "Here are the books that have just come in. They're ready to be put on the shelves, and I thought you'd like to see them first."

"Goodness gracious," Audrey said, then breathed a deep sigh. "Do you really mean it?"

"Why, of course I mean it. Come take a look."

Audrey ran her fingers over the shiny, colorful dustcovers. They were beautiful. So fresh and new. Out of the stack, she chose one novel and one biography.

"I'll take these," she said, suddenly feeling very shy.

"Good choices. Come, let's check them out for you."

After the returned books were checked in and the new ones checked out, Audrey thanked Miss LaVolette. But the thank you seemed paltry. She wished she could explain to this pretty lady just how much her kindness meant.

Audrey hurriedly took her things to the classroom, then went outside since no one was allowed to loiter in the halls until the bell rang. That afternoon, she'd be able to take one of her new books outside and read during recess.

Later, when they were all seated in Mrs. Brumley's classroom, Audrey heard someone say, "Hey, Einstein!"

At first Audrey ignored the voice, but the boy next to her tapped her shoulder. "Hey, brain," he said. "Grace wants you."

She looked around, and Grace pointed to Audrey's desk, where the brand-new library books lay in plain sight. Audrey cringed. She should have put them inside the desk so no one could see them.

"Where'd you get the new books, Audrey Einstein?" Grace whispered. "Do you get special favors at the library?"

"She must be Miss LaVolette's pet," Marie said.

Audrey turned back around to face the front and tried to ignore the chorus as they whispered, "LaVolette's little pet! LaVolette's little pet!" over and over again.

That day in the locker room, *Audrey* was the target.

"Does anyone else in school get nice new library books?" Grace taunted as they were changing into their gym suits.

"Only the brain, Audrey Einstein," Yvette chimed in.

Audrey said nothing, but her face felt hot and her stomach rolled so that she thought she was going to be sick. Later she wondered how she even made it through phys ed class.

That afternoon, she took a book outside with her and sat far from the others under one of the few shade trees on the school grounds. It was the first in the Elsie Dinsmoor series. Miss LaVolette encouraged her to begin the series. "I've ordered the entire set," she said. "They should be arriving next week."

Audrey didn't even notice that the Golden Ring had slipped up behind her, but when she looked up from her book, there they were. All four of them. She noticed their saddle oxfords were getting a little scuffed after a couple weeks of school. Especially Claire Mayer's.

"I think that brand-spanking-new library book should have been mine," Grace said in her lilting voice. "Don't you, girls?"

"I don't see why not," Marie agreed.

Audrey's heart pounded in her head. Why couldn't they just leave her alone? She'd never bothered them.

"But then," Grace went on, "I'm not a little pet." She shook her head and curled up her pretty lip in a mock pout. "I'm not as good as the brain here."

"But you can have the book if you want it, Grace," Marie said, taking a step closer.

Audrey tightened her grip on the book, but it was too late. Before she could think to wrap her arms around it, the book was snatched from her hands.

"Hey!" she said, springing up to her feet. "Give that back!"

"What do you know?" Yvette squealed. "She talks. She really talks."

The four girls laughed and danced around, passing the book one to another while Audrey watched helplessly. Suddenly the bell sounded its ominous clanging. Yvette, who was holding the book, said, "My oh my, time to go." With that, she deliberately dropped the lovely new book into the dirt, tearing the cover and bending the pages.

As the Golden Ring marched smugly away, they were hooking little fingers and laughing. Audrey rescued the book from the dirt and tried her best to wipe the pages clean with the skirt of her dress. Whatever would she tell Miss LaVolette?

Now she knew how Hulda felt when she went home in wet clothes. She guessed having the school librarian for a friend wasn't such a good thing after all.

On Friday night, Jim came to supper at the Harrington house. Having worked on the docks for several years, Jim had rippling muscles and a broad chest. He was a happy guy with a broad smile and a shock of brunette hair that fell across his forehead.

The two lovebirds pushed their chairs close to one another at the table. Every once in a while, Jim would reach over and touch Alice's hand. Audrey thought that would be terribly embarrassing, but it didn't seem to bother Alice one bit.

Seeing them so happy made Audrey feel sad inside. She wanted to be happy for them, but in her own misery, it was difficult to do. That morning she'd intentionally turned around the *i* and the *e* in the spelling word *receive*. She was determined never to get a perfect spelling score again. It was easier and simpler to miss one or two words each week on purpose. And that's exactly what she planned to do.

She wasn't sure how far she'd take her plan, but she could easily write shorter paragraphs in language class and mix up the state capitals in geography. There had to be a way to make the Golden Ring stop making fun of her. The plan to stop doing her best seemed to be the only way.

"But our army is pathetic," Jim was saying to Dad as they ate Mama's delicious pot roast.

Audrey suddenly became aware of the voices swirling around her. They were talking about war again.

Dad nodded grimly. "Pathetic is right. And that doesn't even take into consideration our lack of a fully equipped navy."

"Or the lack of air power," Steve put in.

Audrey cringed at their words. She hated it when the conversation turned to war—as it always seemed to do.

"The totalitarian countries have more than fifteen hundred aircraft," Dad said, waving his fork in the air. "The United States may have about eighty. That's way out of balance."

Not wanting to be left out, Frank added, "Our teacher, Mr. Curtiss, says that Britain has always controlled the seas and will keep on doing so without our help."

Dad shook his head. "But Son, there's more to this than ruling the seas. This war will be won by the nation who rules in the air."

Audrey's father knew exactly what he was talking about. He helped design the airplanes that were being turned out at the Boeing plant. Those fighters and bombers were being shipped to Britain to help defend against the threat of attack from Nazi Germany.

Later they retired to the living room, where they listened to Fulton Lewis Jr., the radio news commentator from Washington, D.C. That meant even more talk about war and serious things.

Audrey went to her room to read a library book.

The next evening, as the family was in the living room after supper, they heard Jim's Ford drive up.

Mother looked up from her knitting. "What are the kids doing coming home at this hour?"

They all knew that on Saturday night the couple never arrived home until around eleven. Even then they would sit out in the Ford talking.

Soon Jim and Alice were standing side by side in the living room doorway, holding hands and looking rather sheepish.

"Mother. Daddy. Everyone." Alice stretched out her left hand. "Jim and I are engaged." But before anyone could react, she added, "And Jim has enlisted in the navy."

Audrey felt as though she'd been hit in the face with a bucket of ice water.

CHAPTER 6
The Lie

Audrey watched as her mother's face turned pale. Everyone froze and the room was dead-still for an endless moment.

The twins were sprawled on their stomachs, coloring in their new coloring books. Suddenly Barb leaped to her feet. "You're gonna be a bride, Alice? A real bride with flowers and a veil and everything?" She ran to hug her sister, breaking the awkwardness of the moment.

Alice gave a nervous laugh. "I don't know about all that, Barb. We've decided to wait to get married."

Mama sighed then. She and Dad were on their feet hugging Alice, shaking hands with Jim, and giving their congratulations.

"You're sure you know what you're doing, son?" Dad asked.

"Oh yes, sir," Jim answered. "Alice and I've talked this over. I want to get into the service now before it all breaks loose."

Dad nodded. Audrey thought her father's eyes looked wet, and he was biting his lip.

Alice looked past Mama and Dad and said, "Well, what about the rest of you? Has everyone turned into zombies?"

Audrey didn't feel like congratulating them at all. Why did they want to get engaged if Jim was going to be leaving? It all seemed so senseless. And so scary. Especially when Jim said, "before it all breaks loose," as if there was no doubt that war was coming. She followed Frank and Isabel in giving hugs and giving her best wishes, but her heart wasn't in it.

Since Steve was still at work, Alice and Jim decided to run over to the Tydol station and tell him their news.

"They have more surprises than *Mystery Theater*," Frank said after they were gone. He went back to his stack of comic books and started reading again.

They all tried to go back to what they were doing, but it was difficult. Dad's newspaper was open again, but Audrey could bet he wasn't reading it.

"Jim's so young to be going away," Mama said with a wistfulness in her voice. The knitting lay untouched on the lamp table beside her.

Dad put down his paper. "I know, Lydia. But if war does come, boys younger than Jim will be called."

"I know. I remember," she said softly.

Of all things, why did Jim have to join the navy? Audrey wondered. Especially now, when German U-boats were shooting torpedoes at everything afloat. She didn't even want to think about it.

Late that night as she lay in bed trying to go to sleep, she could hear Isabel and Alice talking in low voices in their room. The phonograph was playing the wistful strains of "Red Sails in the Sunset." Audrey wondered if Alice were happy or sad. How could her sister bear to let Jim go away?

Audrey didn't return the soiled library book on library day because she didn't want the Golden Ring to see her. Instead, she waited until the next week, when she could go into the library early. The book didn't look all that bad, but there was a tear on the dust jacket.

She tried and tried to think of a way to tell Miss LaVolette what had happened to the book, but nothing seemed right. Being a tattletale was out of the question. She considered returning it and saying nothing, but that seemed terribly ungrateful after the librarian had been so kind to her.

Walking into the library, Audrey lay the book on the desk in front of Miss LaVolette. "Miss LaVolette," she heard herself saying, "do you have any little sisters or brothers?"

Miss LaVolette looked at the book, then looked up at Audrey, her doe eyes all soft and kind. She nodded. "A younger brother."

Audrey pointed to the book. "Well, I have a little sister *and* a brother."

"The twins? Barbara and Edward?"

"That's them," Audrey said, feeling her chest go all tight.

Miss LaVolette smiled. "It happens, Audrey. I know you would never intentionally damage a brand-new book."

"No, ma'am," she answered honestly, "I never would."

Miss LaVolette gave her permission to check out another

book. As she walked out of the library, Audrey told herself that she never actually *said* that the twins did anything. So it wasn't really a lie. Then why did she feel so dirty inside?

Steam rose up in miniature clouds as Audrey smoothed the iron over one of Frank's starched shirts. The steam created a warm mixture of clean-outdoor and laundry-soap smells. There was so much starch in the shirt she practically had to peel it off the ironing board to move it around.

Supper was over, and Mama had set up the iron and ironing board in the kitchen for her. *Fibber McGee and Molly,* one of Audrey's favorite programs, had just come on the radio. Every time Fibber opened a closet door, there was a frightful crashing noise as all the stored junk came tumbling out. Audrey giggled every time it happened.

Isabel told her they used sound effects to make that kind of racket. And Audrey supposed that was true. Nothing was real on the radio or at the movies. Except for the newscasts and newsreels. They were real. And they were scary.

"You're supposed to iron the yoke first." Isabel's voice intruded into her thoughts. "I thought you knew how to iron."

"I *do* know how to iron." Audrey held up the shirt and studied it. It wasn't as good a job as Mama would have done, but it looked good to her.

"Here." Isabel came around to the other side of the ironing board. "Let me show you."

Audrey stepped back out of the way. She hated it when Isabel started acting like she was all grown up. Besides, Audrey was missing the best part of *Fibber McGee and Molly.* At supper, Isabel had accused her of setting the table the wrong way. What was next?

Isabel took the shirt from her. "Like this," she said as

though she were showing Barb how to tie her shoes. "Fold the crease across the yoke and iron the yoke first, then the collar, then the sleeves, then the rest of the shirt, in that order. When you do it right, it won't look like a little kid ironed it."

Audrey took the shirt back from her sister, put it on the hanger, and hung it on the rod with the rest of the dresses, shirts, skirts, and blouses. She looked at the clothes still in the laundry basket, every piece dampened and rolled up tightly to retain the dampness. At the bottom was one of Alice's full skirts. Yards of material to iron. She reached down, picked it up, and held it out to Isabel. "Here," she said. "Show me how to iron this skirt."

Isabel pressed her lips together and squinted up her eyes. "No need to get smart. I was just trying to help."

Audrey said no more, but she didn't see how being bossy could help anyone. She reached over and turned the radio up a little. As long as she listened to the radio programs or read a good book, she could ignore all the unpleasant thoughts that were chasing around in her head.

Just then, Alice came into the kitchen. "Ready for me to start on my half of the ironing?"

Audrey smiled. "I was ready before I started on this." She set the iron on its heel and waved at the full skirt draped over the ironing board.

"I'm surprised you didn't leave it for me." Alice reached out and put her arm around Audrey and gave her a squeeze. "You're a good worker, Audrey," she said, leaning over to plant a soft kiss on Audrey's cheek.

Audrey wanted to tell Alice that Isabel had accused her of being a lazybones, but she didn't think Alice needed to know anyone else's troubles. After all, she had enough on her mind with Jim leaving in two days.

"I'll finish the skirt if you'd like," Alice offered.

"Thanks." Audrey stood a moment, savoring the sweetness of Alice's presence. Surely Alice was dreading Jim's leaving, but her face didn't show it. "Guess I'll go do my homework," Audrey said.

"You do that. We want to see another string of A-pluses just like last year."

Audrey watched a moment as Alice deftly ran the iron over the skirt, smoothing out all the wrinkles. She wanted to tell her sister that this year was nothing like last year and for her not to look for the A-pluses. She wanted to tell her all about the wretched girls in the Golden Ring and about her lie to Miss LaVolette about the torn book. And about the plight of poor Hulda. But she didn't. She turned and went up to her room.

They were all at the train station to see Jim off. All but Dad, who couldn't get off work. Jim was headed for San Diego for his basic training and then off to who knew where. His parents and sister were at the station already, and his mother couldn't stop crying. Alice clung to him. When the conductor called the final "all aboard," Jim almost had to tear himself away from her.

Steam hissed out in a cloud from beneath the wheels as the train began to move. At first the train moved slowly, then the pistons pumped louder as it picked up speed. The whistle sounded a long, loud blast that hurt Audrey's ears. Jim opened the window and was hanging halfway out, waving and waving. And they all waved back until the entire train was gone and an awful silence filled the air.

Back home, Alice went up to her room and shut the door. Not even Isabel could go in. Mother said they were to leave

Alice alone. "She'll come out when she's ready," Mama said.

Audrey knew that feeling. She wished she could shut herself in her room and never come out again.

CHAPTER 7

Back to the Fairfax

October was soggy with rain and heavy with dreary skies. Audrey thought if she had to wear her red boots to school one more day, she'd just die. She hated wearing boots. And she hated staying inside at recess. Staying in at recess meant she couldn't escape the snooty Golden Ring, who seemed to gather power as the school year progressed.

Mama tried to talk her into eating a hot lunch in the lunch room, but Audrey insisted she wanted to walk the twins home. In truth, she wanted to stay away from Queen Anne School just as much as she possibly could.

If the wretched weather wasn't enough, the first report cards were handed out. The sight of B's and B-minuses on Audrey's card nearly made her sick. Mama's reaction was even worse. An awful look of disappointment came over her mother's face as she gazed at the card.

"Audrey, what happened to your A's?" she asked.

"Frank got B's on his card," she said in defense. "Why aren't you upset with him?"

Mama leveled a look at Audrey that made her want to melt away. "Frank's B's are an improvement from the C's he'd been making last year."

Audrey studied her shoe tops as she struggled with the shame and confusion. In order to avoid trouble in class, she had to disappoint her mother. Which was worse? She wasn't really sure.

"Fourth grade is lots harder than third," she said. But that wasn't true. None of it was really hard for her.

"I expect to see you spending more time on homework this next six weeks," Mama ordered.

All Audrey could do was nod her agreement.

A welcome break in the wet weather came the first week of November. Audrey was thankful to be out on the playground again for recess, away from the other kids. She huddled with her coat around her, reading another book in the Elsie Dinsmoor series. Even though the sun was out, the air was chilly. Midway through recess, she was distracted by shouts coming from another part of the playground. It was Hulda again, only this time it was the boys who were tormenting her.

She could hear them saying something about a circus. Putting her finger in her place in the book, she looked over at the commotion. They were playing circus, it seemed, and they'd set up a long two-by-four to serve as the tightrope.

"And here we have my pet bear," one of the boys shouted. Someone had looped a long piece of twine around Hulda's neck. "Come on, bruin," the boy said. "Show the folks how you can walk the high wire."

Hulda stepped up on the two-by-four, but her awkward, clumsy feet simply could not maneuver that board. As she slipped off again and again, the crowd of boys roared with laughter. Why was she allowing them to do that? Why wasn't she yelling at them?

"Roly, poly, big brown bear," they chanted in the midst of the laughter. "Roly, poly, big brown bear."

Audrey closed her eyes to shut out the ugly scene. Where were the teachers? They should stop that cruelty. And why didn't Hulda's parents come to the school and stand up for her?

When she opened her eyes again, she saw that Frank was right in the midst of all the rowdies. And he was laughing! When school let out that afternoon, she was determined to ask him about it. She couldn't believe he would do such a cruel thing.

Although he looked ashamed when she brought it up, he said, "I was only watching them. I sure didn't put that twine around her neck. And the game wasn't my idea."

He glanced over at her as they walked along. "Tell me, do you think I could have stopped them?"

She shook her head. Of course she didn't think that. If he could have stopped the game of circus, then she could have stopped the girls from putting Hulda's clothes in the shower that day. She wanted to tell him that he should have walked away. But what good would that have done? It was so confusing. She didn't know what the answers were for poor Hulda.

"Hulda isn't what really bothers me, anyway," Frank was saying.

At first she wasn't really listening. Then it hit her that Frank was trying to tell her something. Something important. "Something else is bothering you?" she asked.

Frank paused a minute. "The guys I'm friends with, they say bad things about the Japanese. Alan Dreiser said the other day that he hates all Japs. He said his father calls them the yellow peril and that we shouldn't trust any of them."

She waited for him to go on. When he didn't, she said, "A lot of people are saying those things these days." During the times they'd stayed indoors for recess, Audrey heard Grace Farmington say that her father was a member of the America First Committee. He believed that all foreigners were a threat to the nation.

"Whenever I hear them talk like that and I don't tell them that I disagree, I feel I've let Kaneko and Abiko down." His pace slowed a little more. "It's an awful feeling."

Audrey was surprised that Frank was also struggling with problems. "I know what," she said. "Let's ask Mama if we can take the bus to Yesler Way on Saturday. Maybe we can spend time with Kaneko and Abiko. That'd be fun, wouldn't it?"

Frank's face brightened a little. "That *would* be fun. We'll have to get our work done early, though, or Mama won't let us go."

"We can do it," she assured him. Having Frank tell her about his dilemma made her feel a little better about her own problems.

After Mama gave permission for them to go to the Fairfax on Saturday, the twins begged to be able to go along. But Mama said a flat no. Audrey was glad. It would be just her and Frank.

Saturday was overcast, but the rain seemed to be holding off. They boarded the new "trackless trolley," the electric buses that needed no tracks. Unlike the old trolleys, the buses were connected to overhead wires by a long rod. The trackless trolleys were great because they could go places the trolleys never could.

Frank had phoned the evening before to be sure Kaneko and Abiko could spend the day with them. The Wakamutsu boys had to finish their work quickly as well. And they had far more chores at the hotel than Frank and Audrey did at home. There was always sweeping and cleaning to do.

Mr. Wakamutsu was busy at the hotel desk, and Mrs. Wakamutsu was changing linens, so there was no one to tell them to sit down in the kitchen and slowly sip a cup of tea from a handleless cup. Yoshiko and the boys were the ones who met them at the door. Gentle Yoshiko invited them to come and see how Mittens was growing.

"She follows Yoshiko everywhere," Abiko said. "Father says Yoshiko and Mittens are closer than the little Harrington twins."

Frank laughed. "That's mighty close."

Audrey agreed. She couldn't imagine Barb and Eddie not being together.

Yoshiko showed them how Mittens would curl around her neck like a little gray and white collar. "She rides there as I go about my work," Yoshiko said, reaching up to stroke the soft fur. "She likes to be with me."

Audrey wished she could have a kitten of her own. But a kitten at the Harrington household would belong to everyone and not just to her.

"Let's go to the vacant lot," Frank said. "That's what we came for."

They quickly pulled on their jackets and ran out the back door that led into the alley. As they made their way down the alley, they passed warehouses and small manufacturing plants, some of which had window panes broken out.

Audrey pointed to them and asked, "What happened there?"

"Angry Seattle citizens," Kaneko told her.

"What does that mean?" Frank asked.

"Those are Japanese-owned businesses. Like Father was telling you the other day, some people think we're responsible for what the Japanese are doing in China. So they just get mad at all of us."

Audrey shook her head. "That's not right."

Abiko looked over at her, his dark eyes sad. "It's scary, too," he added.

The vacant lot was filled with some of the old friends they used to play with in the neighborhood. A game of kickball was already going, and the four easily joined in. After they tired of kickball, they chose up sides and played Red Rover.

For Red Rover, they created two parallel lines by holding hands tightly. One team would cry out, "Red Rover, Red Rover, send Kaneko right over." At that, Kaneko would run as fast as he could into the line, trying to break it at its weakest point. If he broke through, he went back to his own side. If he was unable to break through, he had to join the opposite side.

It hurt awful when they hit your wrist hard, but everyone was a good sport. When the game was over, they all had sore wrists and cold noses.

It was time to go back to the hotel, grab a snack, and then head to the movies together. It was just like old times.

"What's playing?" Audrey asked as they wolfed down peanut butter and jelly sandwiches.

"*The Wizard of Oz*," Kaneko mumbled around his mouthful of sticky peanut butter sandwich.

"Have you seen it?" Abiko asked.

Audrey shook her head. "We haven't gone to the movies much since we moved. There's a theater in the neighborhood, but it's not right down the street like it is here."

"That's too bad," Kaneko said. His tone made it sound like the most terrible catastrophe imaginable. And to him, it was. Both boys loved the movies.

After washing down their sandwiches with tumblers of iced Kool-Aid, they were out the door again. This time they ran out the front entrance and down the stairs.

"Do you have enough money for candy?" Kaneko asked. He jingled change in his pocket. "Or shall we get popcorn at the theater?"

"Let's do both," Frank suggested. "Let's get Milk Duds at the drugstore and share them, then get two boxes of popcorn at the show and share them."

Kaneko laughed. "What a great plan. Come on. I'll race you."

The four of them ran laughing and panting all the way up Jackson Street to the corner drugstore, where they purchased the Milk Duds. In the middle of the next block was the Palace Theater.

Audrey loved the first warm rush of the aroma of popcorn that met her as she followed the boys inside the lobby. How she wished the Palace was in their new neighborhood. It was in this theater that she first saw great shows like *The Little Colonel,* starring Shirley Temple, and some great Roy Rogers movies. The Palace was a very special place.

After paying their nickels for boxes of popcorn, they filed into the darkened theater and found seats near the front. The place was already packed with noisy kids.

"We'll have the popcorn first," Abiko said, "and save the Milk Duds till last."

As he spoke, the screen lit up and it was time for *Movietone*

News. They told about the new Pan Am Airways plane that was making regular commercial flights to Europe. The plane was called the "Dixie Clipper." People were flying over the Atlantic like they used to take a steamer, only the planes were much faster.

A sports clip showed the fall college football teams in heated games, with cheerleaders in their full skirts leading in rousing cheers.

The scene changed then to Poland, where cameras scanned bombed-out shells of what were once buildings and stores and homes. The sudden takeover of Poland was called a "Blitzkrieg," which meant "lightning war." That's how fast the Nazi army could move. Audrey shivered at the gruesome sights.

The scene changed again and the narrator said, "The Japs show no signs of letting up their militaristic aggression in China."

His tone made the word "Jap" sound as terrible as the word "Nazis."

The scenes showed Japanese soldiers attacking the Chinese island of Hainan. "The strategy of the Japs," said the booming voice, "appears to be to leapfrog from China to the South China Sea. Will they then make a move to take over the entire Pacific?"

Audrey ached inside for Kaneko, Abiko, and the other Japanese kids in the theater. How awful it must be for them to see their own countrymen fighting, killing, and dying.

The afternoon, which had started out being like old times and had been so much fun, was suddenly spoiled.

No matter how much she wanted it, life would never again be like old times.

CHAPTER 8

Audrey Speaks Up

Dad's long hours at the Boeing plant were hard on the entire family. It used to be when the twins acted up and got into mischief, Mama would say, "We'll take care of it when your father gets home." But now the twins were asleep before Dad arrived home.

Every evening they seemed to get in some kind of scuffle. While they once were the same size, Eddie was now getting long-legged and could get the upper hand quickly. That sent Barb crying and wailing to Mama. Audrey had never known them to be so cranky and out of sorts. Mama said it was because they needed their daddy.

Steve used to help with the little ones, but now after he came home from the Tydol station, he had all his homework to do. And Alice was no help at all. As soon as supper was over, she disappeared to her room to write long letters to Jim and listen to "I'll Never Smile Again" and "Red Sails in the Sunset." Their family, it seemed to Audrey, was coming unraveled like the sleeves of Hulda's red cardigan sweater.

Audrey was the one Mama often asked to play with the twins. "Will you keep them occupied until I get this done?" she'd ask.

Without fail, it would come just as Audrey was ready to sit down and get lost in a good book. If she had to change clothes on the Shirley Temple doll one more time, she'd explode.

"Why can't Isabel watch the twins?" she'd say.

"Because," Isabel would answer in her know-it-all voice, "*I'm* helping Mama."

Audrey wanted to say, "I'll help Mama and you play with the twins," but she didn't want to make things any harder for poor Mama. She looked pretty tired as it was.

The wind off Elliott Bay had a bite to it as Audrey walked to school each morning. Brown construction-paper turkeys were taped up in the classroom windows. In their fourth-grade reader, they were reading stories about the Pilgrims and about Squanto, who helped them through the first awful winter. Audrey thought about those brave people who made the journey across the ocean to a new world. Could those children have felt as lonely and empty as she did on this Thanksgiving?

When Alice first announced she planned to spend Thanksgiving day with Jim's family, Audrey was crestfallen. How could her sister even think of leaving them on such a special day. But Mama came to the rescue.

"Our house is big enough," she said to Alice. "Invite them to come have Thanksgiving with us."

At that, Alice's eyes lit up—something that didn't happen much lately. That is, unless the postman brought her a letter from Jim.

What an odd Thanksgiving it was, to have guests who were practically strangers in the house. Mother warned the twins to behave themselves, and they did for a time. But before the pumpkin pie was served, Dad had to take them upstairs and give them a real talking-to. That helped some.

It seemed a shame that Dad was gone so much, and then when he was home he had to scold them. Later Barb called Dad an old meany. Only Audrey heard.

"Dad is not an old meany," Audrey told her little sister. "And if you'd behave, he wouldn't have to scold you so much."

But Barb was too busy pouting to listen. She really could have won a Shirley Temple lookalike contest with that lower lip stuck out.

Jim's parents and sister were nice people. His sister, Janet, worked at the telephone company as a phone operator, and she and Alice were becoming good friends. Still, it just wasn't the same as being with the Wakamutsus.

When the second report cards came out, Audrey took her turn at being scolded by Dad.

"I didn't tell your father the first time," Mama said to her. "I was giving you a chance to bring these grades up." She shook her head in dismay as she studied the card in her hand. "Now I'm afraid I have no choice. I'll have to discuss this matter with him."

So on Saturday morning, when she was usually listening to *Let's Pretend* on the radio, Audrey was in Mama and Dad's bedroom, receiving her scolding. She wanted to agree with Barb—Dad was an old meany.

Why would they get upset with her for bringing home a card full of B's? Well, there was one C in spelling. Perhaps she'd lost track of how many words she'd intentionally missed. She'd have to be more careful next time.

Neither parent asked her what the problem was. Or even if there *was* a problem. All they did was demand that she work harder and get her grades up.

Dad said, "Audrey, your mother and I know you can do better than this. It's important to do your best in everything you do. You understand that, don't you?"

She nodded, but she really didn't understand at all.

At school the next Monday, Mrs. Brumley announced that there would be tryouts for the annual Christmas pageant, which sent whispers rushing around the room like dry leaves in a December wind.

"You'll be Mary," Audrey heard someone saying to Grace. "And the rest of us will be angels."

One of the boys added, "And Hulda will be the donkey."

He said it so loud and there was so much laughter that old Mrs. Brumley actually heard the commotion. "Here, here," she said, tapping the desk with her pencil and peering at them over her small reading glasses. "We'll have no more outbursts. Noisy children will be sent to the principal's office. Do you hear?"

"We hear better than you do," Grace whispered under her breath.

"Dummies," Hulda said.

Stifled snickers spurted out in little bursts. But the hard-of-hearing teacher was oblivious.

Audrey wasn't about to try out for a part. She settled for singing carols with those who didn't receive special parts. As it turned out, a sixth-grade girl was chosen to be Mary. Secretly Audrey was glad. It was about time Grace Farmington learned she couldn't have everything her own way. Grace got the part of an angel, but not all her friends made it. Two members of the Golden Ring wound up as town folk standing around the inn in Bethlehem.

Frank, she learned after school that afternoon, had been selected as the innkeeper. Audrey could tell he was pleased as punch about it, too.

Risers were set up on the stage in the auditorium. A week before the pageant, they began practicing on the stage. Mrs. Marquart, the music teacher, lined them up according to size and the parts they sang. When everyone had their positions, Audrey was on the end of the second row, with Hulda directly behind her. It wasn't pleasant. The girl couldn't carry a tune in a bucket. Every note was off key. It was the worst singing Audrey had ever heard.

Amazingly, Dad was able to take off work for the performance. Audrey wondered if he made a special effort because Frank had such a special part. Or was it because the twins begged him to come? The kindergartners were going to sing "Away in a Manger" as a prelude to the pageant, and both Barb and Eddie were giddy with excitement about being a part of the show, as they called it.

Audrey didn't get to see how well her younger siblings did with their parts. She was with the choir out in the hallway, waiting for their entrance. When the piano began playing "Silent Night," that was their cue to file in. Half of the group came in on one side of the auditorium, half on the other. Up the steps they went onto the stage.

Everything was going fine until they got to the risers. Somehow Hulda's built-up shoe got entangled with the risers or with her other shoe—Audrey was never quite sure which. She saw the big girl start to fall, and then she made the biggest mistake of her life. She reached out to help. As she did, she felt herself being dragged down slowly, slowly, with nothing to grab onto to catch herself or to stop the fall. She heard an awful "oof" as Hulda landed on the boards. Audrey landed unceremoniously right beside her.

"Hey, Goddard," someone whispered, "I thought donkeys were supposed to be sure-footed."

"Tottery-doddery Goddard," whispered someone else.

Mrs. Marquart came running over to see if everyone was all right. A sixth-grade girl whom Audrey didn't even know kindly reached down to give her a hand up. She mumbled her thanks, but her face was burning from embarrassment. With Mrs. Marquart's help, Hulda clumsily got back up on her feet. As she did, she glared at Audrey as though Audrey had been the cause of it all.

"It's all right," the music teacher said with a nice smile. "It could have happened to anyone. As they say on Broadway, 'On with the show.' "

Audrey didn't know how she made it through the rest of the evening. Her ankle ached, and her shin was scraped and raw. But the embarrassment from falling in front of the packed crowd was worse than anything else. Never had she been so humiliated.

Afterward, as they were driving home, Mama said that Audrey had handled herself very well. "I was proud of you," she said.

Then she added, "I feel so sorry for that lame girl. You'd think in this day and age she could have surgery to correct that problem."

But it was Frank and the twins who received all the attention. Frank had been a real hit as the innkeeper, and Dad bent over backward to fuss over the twins, telling them what a good job they'd done. Audrey saw how they basked in his praise.

She wished she'd never seen or heard of Hulda Goddard.

After the pageant, there was yet one more week before Christmas vacation. Audrey could hardly wait. What a welcome break to be away from Queen Anne School from Christmas until after New Year's Day.

The fourth-grade room was festooned with loops and loops of red and green paper chains. Cardboard stars wrapped in tin foil dangled from the ceiling.

Christmas was supposed to be a time of peace and good will, but the Golden Ring didn't seem to know that. They continued to heap up sarcasm and harassment upon poor Hulda. Finally it happened. Audrey had had all she could stomach.

They'd just come into the locker rooms from a rough game of kickball where it seemed everyone in fourth grade wanted to make the ball hit Hulda.

"Hey, tottery, doddery Goddard," Marie Sikes called out. "Step up here on the bench and show us how you took a flying leap at the Christmas pageant."

"Yeah," echoed Yvette. "Show us. We want to see you do it again."

"And get Audrey Einstein to join her," Grace said. "The two of them make a great team."

Audrey was sitting on the bench tying her shoes. Suddenly

she stood up. "Oh, why don't you all just stop it? Don't you ever get tired of hurting people?"

You could have heard a pin drop. Every girl in fourth grade was staring at her like she'd lost her mind. Then Grace began to snicker. Another girl laughed out loud. Pretty soon everyone was laughing at her. She sat back down and finished tying her shoes, but it felt like her face and ears were on fire.

Just then, clumsy Hulda came limping by her on her way out the door. She leaned down and in her thick voice said, "Who asked for your help, little Miss Goody-Two-Shoes? I don't *need* you!"

Audrey stared at the girl as she made her step-roll way out the door of the locker room.

CHAPTER 9

In the Library

Everyone in the Harrington family was overjoyed when Dad announced they would be spending New Year's Eve with the Wakamutsus.

"You mean it, Dad?" Frank said. When Dad assured him that he really did mean it, Frank exploded with a loud "Wahoo!" And Mama had to make him quiet down.

Both Dad and Mama voted that they were to spend their first Christmas in the new house, right there at home. There was plenty of space in the living room for a big tree. The day they brought the tree home and set it up, Alice had received a letter from Jim. Since she was in such good spirits, she pitched in and helped decorate. Even Steve was there to help.

After all the gifts were opened on Christmas morning, they telephoned the Wakamutsus to wish them a Merry Christmas. Audrey thought it was sad that even though they wanted the Wakamutsus to come visit their house on Queen Anne Hill, it wasn't possible. Even though they never discussed it, they all knew it was safer and wiser for Japanese people to stay in their own neighborhood these days. It didn't make any sense, but that's just the way things were.

New Year's Eve came on Sunday, which was perfect. The Tydol station was closed, and Dad was off work. Although Alice would much rather have been with Jim, he was hundreds of miles away. So they all piled into the DeSoto and drove to Yesler Way.

Barb was snuggled on Steve's lap, Eddie was balanced on Isabel's lap, and Audrey had to awkwardly sit on Alice's lap, although she thought she was much too big to do so. Lucky Frank sat up front between Mama and Dad. No one suggested that he sit on anyone's lap.

In spite of the uncomfortable car ride, Audrey thought it was the most perfect New Year's ever. They played games, listened to radio programs, and ate yummy food—both Japanese and American. Games of Monopoly and Parcheesi went on for hours amid laughter and good-natured teasing.

Midway through the evening, the Wakamutsus' preacher and his wife stopped by to give their regards. Audrey remembered the Reverend Patrick Hopkins as one of the regular visitors to the Fairfax when the Harringtons lived there. Pastor Hopkins, a portly man with graying hair and a kind smile, had once been a missionary to Japan. Both he and his wife spoke fluent Japanese.

In fact, when the preacher and his wife spoke in Japanese to Mr. and Mrs. Wakamutsu, their own children could barely understand what the adults were saying.

The extra guests squeezed into the small living area with the rest of them and accepted cups of tea and small cookies. After they'd eaten, Pastor Hopkins asked if he could pray for his parishioners. Audrey quickly learned that the pastor prayed much longer prayers than their own Pastor Colston.

By the time Pastor Hopkins and his wife left, it was nearing midnight. The twins fell asleep and were carted off to one of the bedrooms. Then the mood became more serious.

"It is not only a new year," Mr. Wakamutsu was saying, "but a new decade as well."

"The past decade wasn't a very good one," Steve said, "with the depression, the drought, and the terrible dust storms."

"But the 1930s brought us here to Seattle," Dad put in, "and gave me a great job."

Mama nodded. "There are always blessings if you just look for them."

Audrey wished that were really true. She tried to think of blessings at school, but she couldn't think of any. Well, there was one—Miss LaVolette. But only one!

"Mr. Harrington," said Mr. Wakamutsu, "I have a request to make of you."

"I owe much to you, my friend," Dad replied. "Name your request."

"God forbid that there would ever be war between the country of Japan and our great United States. But should it come to pass, and I am. . ."

Mr. Wakamutsu stopped a moment, and the room grew quiet. Audrey wondered what he thought might happen.

Troubled, he started again. "Should such a state of affairs

come to pass and should something happen to me, might I ask you to watch over our children?"

"I'm sure such a thing would never happen," Dad assured him. "You may not be a citizen, but the entire community knows your reputation as an honest and upstanding person. If it will comfort your mind, however, I give you my word."

"Thank you," Mr. Wakamutsu said, his voice quavering. "Thank you so very much." He lifted up his cup of tea. "To the 1940s. May they be good to all of us."

The grown-ups lifted their cups of tea, and the children lifted their glasses of Coca-Cola. "To the forties," they echoed and drank a toast.

"While I would like to toast to peace," Dad said, "it would seem there is no peace anywhere in the world tonight. So I pray that during this terrible time, people would come to know the Prince of Peace."

Mama touched Dad's arm. "I think that's a prayer, not a toast."

Dad blushed. "I suppose you're right, Lydia. I'm not much at this toasting business."

"Then we shall pray," said Mr. Wakamutsu. "Pray that no matter what happens, God will be our protector and our guide."

"Amen to that," said Alice.

They all knew her mind was on Jim.

Just as Dad closed his prayer, the melody of "Auld Lang Syne" came over the radio. Smiling, Mama joined in on the chorus, "For auld lang syne, my dear. . ."

Dad's baritone blended with her soprano, "For auld lang syne. . ."

Then they all joined in. "We'll take a cup o' kindness yet, For auld lang syne." Mama and Dad knew the words to all the verses, and their voices blended beautifully together. As the last strains faded away, they all shouted, "Happy New Year!" It was officially 1940.

The morning Audrey returned to school following holiday break, she arrived early and hurried downstairs to the library. Except for the books she'd received as Christmas gifts, she'd had no new books to read for over a week.

"Welcome back, Audrey." Miss LaVolette's voice was as cheery as ever. "I've been thinking about you over vacation time."

"About me?" Audrey placed her books on the desk.

"About you. Since you're such a book lover, how would you like to work here in the library with me?"

At first Audrey thought she might be teasing. Growing up in a big family, Audrey was used to teasing. And Miss LaVolette's invitation seemed almost too good to be true.

"When would you want me to work?" she asked.

"It's winter now, and the weather will be messy outside— would you mind giving up two afternoon recesses a week?"

Now she knew Miss LaVolette was serious. She would gladly give up every recess and phys ed class to boot. "Oh yes," Audrey said, letting the excitement soak deep inside her. "I'd love to help."

How fun it would be to be among the stacks of books, helping to log them and put them away. But then another thought hit her. What would the Golden Ring say about this? It would give them just one more thing for them to torment her about.

"What is it, Audrey?" Miss LaVolette was studying her face. "Is something wrong? Perhaps it's not such a good idea. Perhaps I'm asking an awful lot."

Phooey on the Golden Ring. What did they know anyway? She'd taken all their rude remarks before. "Nothing's wrong,

Miss LaVolette. Nothing at all. When do I start?"

The librarian smiled as she pulled the cards from the card file to check in Audrey's returned books. "As soon as I clear it with Mrs. Brumley and the principal," she said.

By the next week, Audrey was slipping out of the classroom at the beginning of recess to go work in the library. Miss LaVolette taught her how to put books on the shelves in proper order and how to file the cards correctly in the wooden card files. Together they decorated the bulletin board in the hallway outside the library. Just being among all the books would have been joy enough, but to work with Miss LaVolette was next to heaven.

The reactions from the Golden Ring to Audrey working in the library came soon enough. "LaVolette's little pet," was whispered in the classroom. That wasn't too bad. But in the locker room one day, it took a different twist.

"Were *you* asked to work in the library?" Grace asked someone. As usual, Audrey stayed as far away from the Ring as she could and kept her back turned as well.

"Why, no," came the reply. "Were you?"

"Me? Of course not. I'm not anyone's pet."

"Why do you think the new girl and the new librarian are so buddy-buddy?"

"I don't know."

Audrey's shoe lace was in a knot. As her heart pounded, she fumbled to get it loose so she could get out of there.

"Maybe because they're both Jap lovers," came the unmistakable voice of Grace Farmington. The statement brought gasps from the others.

"Audrey Einstein is a Jap lover?" Yvette's shrill voice asked.

"She used to *live* with Japs," Grace said, her voice filled with disdain. "What do you think of that?"

Audrey's other shoe was on and tied, and she almost ran out of the locker room. Her palms felt all sweaty, and her mouth felt like it was stuffed with cotton balls. The Golden Ring was shooting at her with both barrels. Was there no mercy?

Alice was practically flying around the house. She sang and whistled and laughed as she urged the rest of the family to help get the house spotless. Jim would be home for a week's leave before being shipped out.

When she first read his letter, which gave the details, Alice's face had turned pale. "The Philippines? Jim's being sent to the Philippine Islands." She stared at the letter in her hand.

"He had to be sent somewhere," Mama had said in her gentle voice. "You didn't think he'd be sitting in California for his tour of duty."

"No, of course not." Alice folded the letter then and put it away. "Well, he's going to be home for a few days. And we're going to make the best of it."

That's when the cleaning binge began. The only trouble was that everyone was supposed to be involved. Even Isabel balked. Audrey had seldom seen Alice and Isabel get into a fuss. But this was one time they did.

Isabel told her older sister to stop bossing her around. And Alice accused Isabel of not caring about this most important event in her life. It sounded rather childish to Audrey, who stared at her sisters in disbelief. Mama finally had to step in and calm them down.

"Alice, you're overwrought, my dear," Mama told her. "We all know this is a trying time for you, but you can't take it out on others."

"I was only asking for help!" Alice said, and with that she burst into tears and ran up to her room.

Isabel just shrugged her shoulders.

Audrey wished she could make Isabel understand that she was ten times more bossy than Alice ever thought about being. But Audrey didn't want to make matters worse.

Alice asked for some days off work when Jim came home. She said she didn't care if she got fired. She was going to spend every moment possible with her fiancé. Of course, she didn't get fired. In fact, her boss at the shipping firm told her he was proud of Jim for joining up. He gave her the entire week off.

Mama, Isabel, Audrey, and Alice were in the kitchen getting the special welcome-home supper prepared when they heard the Ford turn in. Alice went flying out the back door. Audrey was sure her sister's feet never touched the steps. Audrey ran to the window just in time to see Jim jump from his car, grab Alice, and swing her round and round. When they stop twirling around, he leaned down and kissed her—it seemed like forever. Mama said for her to get away from the window, but Isabel was staring, too, so she didn't move.

When Jim came in the back door with Alice, Audrey couldn't believe it was the same person. He was dressed in his navy blue bell-bottom trousers and loose fitting shirt, with a white sailor hat perched jauntily on his head. His hair was cut short, and he stood ramrod straight. Tall and proud. It took Audrey's breath away. He never looked that handsome when he was just a longshoreman on the docks. How would Alice ever be able to say good-bye to him a second time?

CHAPTER 10

Quiz Contest

Audrey was right. Saying good-bye to Jim a second time was devastating for Alice. She didn't talk as much as she used to. She didn't smile much, either. Audrey thought her oldest sister shouldn't be sitting around listening to "I'll Never Smile Again" on the phonograph over and over again. But no one was asking Audrey's opinion.

After a couple weeks, Alice volunteered for the "Bundles for Britain" relief work, which kept her away from home more than ever. That meant she wasn't there to help with the bushel baskets of ironing anymore. Alice said it was important that she be involved in humanitarian work since she was engaged to a sailor on a warship.

Isabel said that ironing for the family was humanitarian, but Mama told her to hush. Audrey tended to agree with Isabel on that point. It seemed to Audrey that Alice should do her fair share whether she was helping send supplies to Britain or not.

One Saturday afternoon when much of the housework was finished, Audrey was headed to her room to finish a library book. As she passed the bedroom of her older sisters, Isabel called out, "Hey, Audrey. Come here a minute."

Audrey stopped in her tracks. "Are you talking to me?"

Isabel laughed. "Know any other Audreys that might happen to be in our upstairs today?"

Audrey laughed, too. "I guess not." She stepped inside. The older girls' room always smelled nice, like Evening in Paris and To a Wild Rose body powder. The phonograph was vibrating with a swing number played by Tommy Dorsey's orchestra. Both Alice and Isabel liked the sound of the swing bands. Audrey wondered if Isabel had permission to use it while Alice wasn't there.

Isabel was sitting at the dressing table brushing her hair in an upward sweep. "What do you think?" She turned around while holding the hair up off her neck. "Do I look older?"

"A little bit." Audrey sat down on the bed. Actually she didn't think the hairdo made her sister look any different at all.

"Audrey, do you think Mama would ever let me go on a date?"

Audrey was shocked. "A date?"

"Oh, not a real date like in a car. But maybe to go with a boy to the drugstore after school for a malt?"

Audrey hadn't the slightest idea what Mama might say. Nor did she have the slightest idea why Isabel would be asking her, of all people. "I guess all you can do is ask," she offered lamely.

Isabel turned back around to face the mirror. "You're probably right." She let the handful of hair drop and began brushing it again. "I know I'm not as pretty as some of the girls in school, but there's this boy. Randall is his name. Well, he started talking to me. Our lockers are next to each other." Isabel smiled as though they were sharing a good secret. "It's a swell way to get to know each other."

Audrey wasn't sure how to answer, but she tried to think of something so Isabel wouldn't stop talking to her. "That *is* a great way. We don't have lockers in grammar school."

"Well, you will in junior high. Sometimes having a locker is a pain in the neck. But when a nice boy has the one next to you, it can be a good thing."

Audrey was thinking that with her luck, she'd have a locker next to Grace Farmington.

"Anyway," Isabel went on, "he's asked me if I'd share a malt with him after school some day."

"Did he say which day?"

Isabel shook her head. "Just *some* day." She got up from the dressing table and did a few dance steps as she came across the room. "I'm learning to dance. One of the girls at school knows how to do the boomps-a-daisy. She's teaching me."

Audrey nodded, trying to look as though she were old enough to truly be sharing this conversation when she really wasn't. She'd never heard of such a thing as boomps-a-daisy.

Isabel sat down beside her on the bed and reached out to touch Audrey's shoulder-length hair. It was as though Isabel were looking at her, truly looking at her, for the very first time.

"Are you going to wear your hair straight like this forever?"

Audrey shrugged. "I'm not as good as you are with hairdo ideas."

"Have you thought about cutting it? Then you can pin it up in pin curls and it would be fluffed around your face."

Audrey gave a little shiver. It sounded wonderful. "I don't even know *how* to make pin curls."

"Nothing to it." Isabel gave a wave of her hand. "You just take a strand like this." She lifted a strand of her own hair. "Then you wrap it around your first finger like this." She chuckled. "It's a little easier when it's wet and has some Dep on it. When it's all wound, you pull your finger out, hold the curl in place, and put in the bobby pins."

She demonstrated by opening a bobby pin with her teeth and then slipping it over the pin curl. Another bobby pin was put in to form an X on the curl and she was finished. "It's that simple."

Audrey had seen both Alice and Isabel with their hair all up in pin curls, but neither of them had ever taken the time to show her how to do it.

"Do you think Mama would let me get my hair cut?"

Isabel jumped off the bed. "As you just told me, all you can do is ask."

Mama said yes to both girls. Isabel was allowed to stop at the drugstore with Randall, but only once a week and only for forty-five minutes. Isabel was delighted. And Audrey was delighted that she was going to get her long hair cut off. Now Mama couldn't look at her and say, "Audrey, why don't you go braid your hair?"

With her hair shorter and curlier, Audrey felt different somehow. She knew the girls at school wouldn't treat her any differently, but that didn't really matter. When she looked in the mirror, she liked what she saw. Even Steve complimented her on how it looked.

Her arms got tired sometimes when she was putting up her pin curls each night. Especially the ones in the back. But she wouldn't complain. She figured it was part of growing older. Lucky Barb. Her hair was so curly she'd never need pin curls.

On a morning in mid-March, Audrey entered the front hall of the school and saw an entire set of encyclopedias sitting on a long table. Above the set of books hung a big sign that read, "Win a Set of Encyclopedias. Quiz Contest, April 19th."

Audrey had no idea what a quiz contest was, but she soon found out. Mrs. Brumley handed out forms that explained the details. The contest was for fourth, fifth, and sixth graders. Those entering the contest were to answer questions ranging from geography and history to grammar and arithmetic. The contest, it said, was to be held in the school auditorium. And the grand prize was the set of encyclopedias.

For a brief moment, Audrey considered filling out the form and entering the contest. How she would love to have that set of books on the shelves of the Harrington living room. But remembering the last attack from Grace and her little group, she felt it wasn't really worth it. Who needed any more grief? She folded up the paper, stuffed it into her desk, and put it out of her mind.

Her birthday was right around the corner, and she was excited about finally turning ten. That was a much more pleasant thought that any old quiz contest.

A few days before the big day, Mama and Isabel asked her if she wanted to invite any of her friends over for a little party.

Audrey hesitated. She wasn't sure what to say. Mama and Isabel glanced at one another. How could she tell them she didn't have even one friend at Queen Anne School? Mama had always preached to them that to have a friend you must be one. She sure didn't want to be accused of not being a good friend.

And Isabel was always telling her that she hid behind her books. "You need to stop reading so much and have a little fun," she'd say.

So when they asked about inviting friends, she shook her head. "Thanks for the offer, but I'd rather be with family."

"All right," Mama said. "It's your birthday."

Mama outdid herself in baking a high, light angel food cake with pink seven-minute frosting fluffed all over it. She topped it off with ten pink candles.

There were several brightly wrapped gifts sitting on the sideboard in the dining room. Audrey could hardly wait for dinner to be over so she could open them. But first they had to light candles, and then everyone sang "Happy Birthday" to her.

"Should we wait until your father gets home before opening gifts?" Mama asked with a twinkle in her eye.

"No, no," the twins called out in unison as though the gifts were theirs. "We'll be asleep before Daddy gets home."

But Audrey knew Mama was teasing, and soon the twins knew it as well. The little ones were in charge of bringing the gifts to her. The first gift was a pair of brand-new roller skates. She'd been using old ones that had belonged to Alice and Isabel. Now she had a pair all her own.

The next gift was shaped like a shoe box. Sure enough, inside the wrapped box was a pair of black-and-white saddle oxfords.

Isabel smiled. "I told Mama to get them for you," she said. "Everyone's wearing them this year."

As if Audrey didn't know. She lifted them up and inhaled the good smell of new shoe leather.

The last package, which was signed from all her brothers and sisters, was the best of all. Two pairs of dungarees. Blue denim dungarees just like the girls in the Golden Ring wore every Friday—with their pant legs rolled up just above the top of their socks. Audrey hugged the dungarees to herself and laughed right out loud. What a wonderful gift.

"Thank you, everybody. Thanks so much." And she went around hugging everyone. Even Frank, who said he was ready for a second piece of cake!

Audrey felt great wearing her dungarees and new saddle oxfords to school on Friday. And of course, Friday was library day, so it was a double-good day. When Miss LaVolette saw her, she raised her eyebrows and grinned. "You look great," she said softly so no one else could hear.

Audrey thanked her as though it were the most natural thing in the world to receive such a compliment. Inside she was turning cartwheels. As usual, she grabbed a couple books, headed to the reading area, and sat down at one of the tables where she could be alone. Later, she sensed that someone was nearby browsing the magazine racks where the *Jack & Jill* and *Wee Wisdom* magazines were kept.

Then she heard a voice say, "Audrey Harrington, for being an Einstein, you sure are dumb."

Audrey turned around and looked straight at Hulda Goddard.

CHAPTER 11

Take Me Out to the Ball Game

Audrey was shocked. Hulda hardly ever talked to her. And now that she had, she'd called her dumb. What was going on? She turned back to her book and ignored the remark.

Once again came Hulda's grating whisper. "You are so dumb." Audrey glanced up at the girl again. She was flipping through an old issue of *Jack & Jill*, acting as though nothing had happened. Audrey went back to her book.

"You're dumb to let all those snobs tell you how to act. I don't let them tell me how to act, and you're smarter than I am by a long shot." Audrey heard the magazine hit the shelf as

Hulda put it back. "You're so dumb to let those silly girls cheat you out of a set of encyclopedias."

She stepped closer to where Audrey was sitting, the shuffle of her built-up shoe sounding on the wooden floor. "You're the only one in fourth grade who could really show 'em up," she said as she walked on by. "Why don't you do it?"

Over the weekend, Audrey had a lot of time to think about Hulda's remark. It was true. She lay awake thinking about it. Why had she allowed those girls to force her into missing spelling words? And let her schoolwork slide? And get bad grades—all on purpose?

Just so they wouldn't make fun of her? They made fun of her anyway. No matter what she did. For the first time, Audrey saw this was a losing battle. So why continue to battle? Hulda never changed being who she was just to please the Golden Ring.

During her next worktime in the library, Audrey asked Miss LaVolette, "What would a person have to study to be able to compete well in the quiz contest?"

Miss LaVolette's eyes lit up. "Have you entered?"

"Not yet. I'm just thinking about it."

"I was hoping you would. It'd be a good experience for you. A student who reads as much as you do already has a broad knowledge in a number of areas." She pulled out a pencil and said, "Tell you what. While you do the filing, I'll make a list of a few books that might help." Then she asked, "Do you have someone at home who would help ask you questions?"

Audrey smiled. "I have a whole houseful."

"Oh, one more thing." Miss LaVolette reached over to the corner of her desk and handed her a form. "Be sure and enter!"

Every week, Mrs. Brumley gave a practice spelling test on Wednesday and the graded test on Friday morning. Anyone who made a perfect score on Wednesday opted out of the Friday test. Audrey made up her mind that from then on until school was out, she was going to try to make a perfect score on every practice test. Just like that, she decided to stop failing on purpose. And it felt so good! Wait until Mama and Dad saw her next report card.

When she made a perfect score on the Wednesday test, the whispers started fast and furious. But this time it didn't really matter. Like Hulda said, why should she let those girls tell her how to act? God gave her a brain, and she was going to use it.

At home, Audrey began to study like crazy, using the books that Miss LaVolette suggested. She pestered Mama, Frank, and Isabel to ask her questions. When one got tired, she turned to the next. Mama seemed pretty happy that her daughter was serious about her studies again.

"I really want to win that set of encyclopedias," she told Isabel one evening. They were sitting on Isabel's bed, and Isabel was asking her questions out of a history book. Ever since their talk when Isabel had told her about Randall, Isabel had started talking to her more. She even told her details of what Randall was like and how much fun they had at the drugstore.

Isabel might have been lonely because Alice was gone so much. Audrey didn't care what the reason was, she was just glad Isabel was no longer treating her like a baby.

"You're going to be competing with kids two years older than you are," Isabel reminded her as she scanned the questions.

"I know," Audrey said. "I haven't forgotten. But I still want to win the encyclopedias."

Isabel laughed. "I guess it's good to have a goal."

Audrey had barely a month to prepare, and she was determined to make the most of every second.

With the arrival of spring came more bad news from Europe.

Hitler had overrun Denmark and taken over Norway, and the German army did it with such speed and surprise that neither country could mount a defense.

Audrey watched her father's face grow serious as he listened to the radio news and discussed the war with Mama. He would shake his head in bewilderment and say, "I don't see how we can stay out of it much longer."

Dad was pleased when Neville Chamberlain was no longer prime minister of Britain. When Winston Churchill took his place, Dad said, "Now things will change for the better." Audrey sure hoped that was so.

Spring also brought with it complications in Frank's breathing problems. Sometimes Audrey could hear him coughing in the night. Hard, deep coughing. She wished she could do something to help. It must be awful to have such trouble breathing.

Mama was always telling him to be careful. Not to overexert. Not to get overtired. And on and on. But he never listened. Audrey watched him at recess, and he played just as hard as all the other boys in the ball game. But she'd never tell Mama.

Steve was also getting baseball fever. He kept saying he was going to get tickets to one of the Rainiers' home games. Audrey never dreamed that might include her.

One night at supper he said to her, "Hey, little sister, do you think you could take one Saturday afternoon off from your new study binge?"

"I don't know," she answered. "Why?"

Steve gave her an impish grin and winked. "I finally have tickets to the Rainiers' game."

"Hey," Frank spoke up. "You were gonna take *me* to that game, not her."

"Well, actually, Frank, I'm taking both of you."

Audrey thought surely she must be dreaming. She'd wake up in a minute and her brother would say he was only teasing. Could it be that Steve was actually taking *her* to a ball game?

"And that's not all," Steve added. "We're taking Kaneko and Abiko as well."

That set Frank to cheering. "Steve, you're the best brother ever in the whole world."

But just like a boy, instead of Frank giving Steve a hug, the two of them started wrestling right in the middle of the kitchen. Mama made them stop. "Before you break something," she said. But she was smiling when she said it.

To keep peace in the family, Mama planned to take the twins to the zoo at Woodland Park the same afternoon. Isabel, it turned out, had a day-long baby-sitting job for a family up the street.

Since it had rained all week, Audrey was beginning to wonder if the game would be rained out. As Saturday grew nearer, she found herself praying for good weather. Sure enough, when she opened her eyes on Saturday morning, welcome sunshine was pouring in their bedroom windows.

"I'm gonna see bears today," Barb said as soon as she woke up. Audrey was glad her little sister was happy about going to the zoo. Mama said the twins would never be able to sit still through a whole ball game.

"You're not leaving to go to the zoo until after lunch," Audrey informed her as she crawled out of bed. "We all have to pitch in and help clean house this morning."

Barb stopped and thought about that a minute. "It's a long time till lunch," she replied, sounding a little disappointed.

For once Audrey agreed with Barb—it did seem like a long time. And she didn't like having to clean house when Alice and Isabel were both gone.

By the time Steve came home from the station at lunchtime, though, Frank and Audrey were all ready to go. The three of them headed for the bus stop a few blocks from their house. As they waited, Frank and Steve started singing "Take Me Out to the Ball Game." Audrey looked around to see if anyone was within hearing distance.

Buy me some peanuts and Cracker Jacks.
I don't care if I never get back.

Then instead of being embarrassed, Audrey joined in until they were laughing so hard they had tears in their eyes.

As they boarded the bus, Audrey made sure Steve sat between them. Without her sisters along, it was almost like having Steve all to herself. She didn't mind that as they bounced along, Frank and Steve talked on and on about Rainiers players and the details of how they'd won the pennant last spring. Sitting there in the bus with the warm sun streaming in on her face, a warm glow of peace and contentment started at the top of her head and trickled all the way to her toes. She could have ridden that bus forever.

Since the ball park was south of Yesler Way, the Wakamutsu boys would catch another bus and meet them at the front gate. The gates hadn't opened when they stepped off the bus, but a noisy, happy crowd had already gathered.

"How'll we find Kaneko and Abiko in all these people?" Frank asked.

"We'll find them," Steve promised. "Just as long as they wait by the gate, we'll find them." He closed his big hand over Audrey's. "Let's just make sure we don't get separated from one another."

Audrey felt safe and secure with Steve holding onto her.

"If we don't see them by the time we get to the turnstile," Steve said, "we'll just step aside and wait a few minutes."

As soon as the gates opened, the crowd moved rather quickly. When they approached the turnstiles, the boys were waiting for them.

"Wow," Frank said. "You must have camped here all night."

Kaneko grinned. "Abiko here was determined we'd be the first ones in line."

Steve chuckled at their exuberance. "Come on troops." He waved them forward like a scout leader. "Let's go to the ball game."

Audrey couldn't remember a more wonderful day. She laughed and cheered and booed and shouted at the umpires right along with the boys. They downed hot dogs on soggy buns and ate boxes of sweet Cracker Jacks and drank ice cold Nehi pop from drippy wet bottles. The dust in the air caused Frank to have one good coughing fit, but it didn't last long and he seemed to be okay. If it got bad enough, they'd have to go home. Audrey wouldn't have liked that at all.

The Rainiers were strutting their stuff in this first home game of the season. By the top of the seventh, they were leading, seven to three. The boys were ready to take a trip to the restroom.

"You going with them?" Steve asked Audrey.

"Guess I better." She stood up and stretched her legs.

Steve tipped up his bottle of Nehi, draining the last, then said, "I'll stay here and fill you in on what happens."

"Great," Frank said. "Come on. I'll lead the way."

They filed down the stairs to the lower level. The boys went one way, and Audrey went the other. "Promise you'll wait for me right here," she said.

"Promise," Abiko told her.

She sure didn't want to have to find their seats by herself.

A few minutes later, when she came out of the cool, dark restroom area, Audrey squinted against the sunshine. Shading her eyes, she saw the boys standing at the stairs. They'd stationed themselves where they could watch the game and wait for her. As she moved to go toward them, she felt someone grab her arm.

"Hey, you," said a boy's voice.

Yanking her arm free, she whirled around to see two boys from Frank's class at school. One was Alan Dreiser, who had a curly mop of sandy hair. The other, Jack Kendrick, was a little shorter and dark complexioned.

"You're Frank Harrington's sister, right?" Alan asked, leaning toward her.

She nodded. These were the boys Frank played baseball with every recess. But they looked angry. "If you want to talk to him, he's right there." She pointed down the walkway toward Frank.

"We see him," Jack said through clenched teeth. "Him and his two Jap buddies."

Audrey bit her lip and stood stone-still, although she wanted to run away as fast as she could.

"We didn't know he was a Jap lover." Alan clenched and unclenched his fists. "He never told us his little secret."

Jack bumped her arm. "You tell him for us. Tell him we know. And tell him he'd better watch out. We're out to teach him a lesson."

They turned and walked away.

CHAPTER 12

Frank's Fight

Tears burned in Audrey's eyes as she stood there a moment. How could people be so hateful and mean? Those two boys sounded like the girls in the Golden Ring. She had no idea if she were going to tell Frank, or if she did, how and when she would do it.

For now, it was important to pretend nothing had happened. That would be hard because she was shaking from head to toe. Frank still hadn't seen her, so she slipped back into the restroom, splashed cold water on her face, and dried off on the linen towel, pulling it around and around until she found a clean place. Then she stopped and took a deep breath.

"Brother," Frank said when she stepped up beside them. "I wondered if you were gonna take all day."

"Yeah, we were about ready to send Abiko in to get you," Kaneko said. And they all giggled. Audrey included.

The Rainiers handily won their game, and Audrey tried to keep on cheering as she'd done before, but for her, the afternoon was spoiled. She couldn't stop thinking about the boys' threats. What were they planning to do to Frank?

Her silence at supper wasn't noticed. The twins were going on and on about bears, elephants, and lions they'd seen. Eddie could barely eat for demonstrating the roar of a lion. He even showed them how the elephants sucked peanuts up through their trunks. Mama kept telling him to calm down, but it didn't faze him.

And Frank described the winning home run, which was slammed with the bases loaded, bringing all the runners safely into home plate. Even Isabel had had a great day with her little charges and enjoyed telling stories of how cute and well behaved they were.

Meanwhile, Audrey was plotting a moment when she could privately tell Frank what had happened. After she and Isabel finished washing and drying the supper dishes, she went to her room to try to study for the quiz contest. She fluffed the pillows and propped herself up in her bed. On her lap was a fifth-grade language book that Miss LaVolette had let her borrow out of the library. She was determined to learn the parts of speech and be able to identify them in sentences, but it was hard to keep her mind on her work. From down in the living room she could hear the beginning of *Your Hit Parade* coming on the radio.

Just then, Frank passed by her door with Steve's small Silvertone radio in his hands, the electrical cord trailing behind him.

"Frank!" she called out.

He stopped and stuck his head in the door. "Yeah?"

"Where're you going?"

"Steve said I could borrow his radio tonight. He's gone riding with some of his friends. I'm going to listen to the programs I like, not the boring old *Hit Parade*." He paused a minute. "Hey, want to take time out from your brain-strain to join me?"

It was perfect. She lay aside the book and hopped up. "I'd love to." She could learn the parts of speech Sunday afternoon.

He set the radio on his bedside table and got down on his hands and knees to locate the outlet.

"Rinso Blue gets your clothes white!" came the loud voice from the radio. Frank grabbed the dial to turn it down. "Don't need it that loud," he said with a grin.

As he was turning the dial from station to station, Audrey sat down on the rug beside him. "Did I tell you I saw two of your friends at the ball game?"

He turned around to look at her, a strange expression on his face. "You didn't say anything about it. Who'd you see?"

"Alan Dreiser and Jack Kendrick."

Frank swallowed hard. The radio was still giving out static since the station wasn't tuned in clearly. "Did they see me?"

She nodded.

"And?"

"They called you a Jap lover."

He turned back to the radio and busied himself with the dial. All of a sudden the sounds of breaking glass and a police siren blared from the radio, followed by a burglar alarm, machine guns rat-a-tat-tatting, and tires squealing. They both jumped. It was the beginning of *Gangbusters*. Frank grabbed at the knob to turn it down a little.

When he acted as though he were totally engrossed in the *Gangbusters* show, she added, "They said something else, Frank."

"Yeah?" He wouldn't look at her.

"They said they were going to teach you a lesson."

"Don't worry," he said. "I can take care of myself."

His voice didn't sound too sure. Audrey suddenly felt sorry for him. He, too, had tried to fit in at Queen Anne, and now this. She could tell he didn't want to talk about it anymore, so she sat with him and they listened to all their favorite programs until time to go to bed.

The entire day was gone, and she hadn't studied at all. April 19 was drawing closer and closer. She wasn't sure if she was ready for the contest. How was she to know if she'd studied enough? At least the other kids had experienced the contest before, and some had been entrants. But to her it was all brand new.

In the night, she heard Frank coughing and heard Mama getting up with him. Audrey had heard Mama say once that his coughing always got worse when Frank became excited or upset. Audrey was sure Frank was upset over what she'd told him.

The sermon the next morning at church was taken from the Sermon on the Mount. When Pastor Colston talked about doing good to those who persecute you, Audrey thought about all the persecution against the Japanese in Kaneko and Abiko's neighborhood. She thought of the persecution she'd received at school and the way Hulda was treated. Even Frank's friends were mad at him simply because he was friends with two Japanese boys.

It didn't seem possible that you could always do good to people who said mean things against you. But then, Pastor Colston reminded them that Jesus knows that no one is capable of keeping all the instructions in the Bible.

"It was never God's plan for us to be good in and of ourselves," Pastor told his congregation. "That's why Jesus came and died. When we ask Jesus into our hearts, He not only brings the gift of salvation, He also equips us to follow His example and His instructions."

Audrey glanced over at Frank to see if he were listening. He was playing tic-tac-toe with Eddie on the border of his Sunday school paper. It seemed to her that he really should be paying attention. This was pretty important stuff.

That night Audrey prayed for Jesus to help her to be good to the girls in the Golden Ring and to help Frank be good to the boys who were angry at him.

Monday afternoon, Audrey was on the playground during recess and saw that Frank was sitting on top of the jungle gym all by himself. The ball game was going on without him. She wanted to go to him and tell him she knew how he felt, but that would only make it worse. He wouldn't want the boys to think he needed a girl to help him out.

Audrey was determined to stick close by Frank as they walked to and from school each day and watch to see that nothing happened. For two days nothing happened. Frank was a little more glum than usual, but at least no one tried to hurt him. She was beginning to think Alan and Jack had made empty threats—that is, until Wednesday afternoon.

Audrey had stayed behind a minute to get another study book from Miss LaVolette. By the time she got outside, Frank was way ahead of her. As she was hurrying to catch up with him, she saw Alan and Jack step out in front of him on the sidewalk. Fear crawled over her in prickly waves. She wished Pastor Colston would appear to tell Frank how to be good to those bullies. She slowed down and tried to sneak around through front yards, crouching behind privet hedges.

When she came up to them, she heard Jack saying something like, "What do you have to say for yourself, Jap lover?"

"If I were you, *I* sure wouldn't be seen in public with them," Alan added.

"We don't like Jap lovers, do we, Alan?"

"No sir, Jack. We don't like 'em one little bit."

Peering through the hedge, Audrey could see they were moving closer to Frank. She didn't know whether to scream for help or run home to get Mama. Just then, Alan grabbed Frank's arms, and Jack reared back his fist for a hard punch.

A scream froze in Audrey's throat as she saw Frank convulse into a heavy coughing spasm and go limp.

CHAPTER 13
Jujitsu

"Lay him flat," Audrey yelled as she jumped out from behind the hedge.

"We didn't *do* anything! Honest!" Alan said. His eyes were wide.

"Lay him out flat on his back," she ordered again. Frank's intermittent wheezing was punctuated by spasms of coughing. His face was growing redder by the minute.

The two did as she said, then they started to slip away. She stood up and glared at them. "Oh no you don't. You're both going to help me get him to the house. After he's rested a minute, that is."

"Not me," Jack said.

"Grab him and help," Alan ordered. "This was all your idea in the first place."

Audrey made them wait until Frank's breathing was back to normal. She'd seen Mama do the same thing plenty of times. Then she had them hook his arms over their shoulders. Frank just sort of stumbled along. When they were almost to the house, Frank realized what was going on. He shook the boys loose, and they took off like scared rabbits.

Frank turned to Audrey with a pained look. "You better not tell Mama a word of this," he warned.

"You can trust me." She helped him the rest of the way up the walk. Mama met them at the door.

"What happened?" she demanded.

"Just a little coughing spell on the way home," Audrey told her.

Mama shook her head. "You were overdoing again, weren't you, Frank? I've told you again and again not to over-do. And we have no more of Mrs. Wakamutsu's herbal tea."

She helped Frank into the living room and made him lie down on the couch. "Audrey, I'll call Mrs. Wakamutsu, and you take the bus to go get it just in case Frank has another attack in the night."

When Mama got off the phone, she said, "The boys will meet you in front of Walgreen's Drugstore at Fifth and Virginia."

Audrey knew that was right in the middle of downtown.

"She insisted that you not make the trip all the way to the

Fairfax by yourself. And," Mama added, handing her money for the remedy, "make sure the boys take the money."

Audrey dropped the money into her pocket. She knew there wasn't anything wrong with making the trip to the hotel by herself. It's just that Mrs. Wakamutsu was so very polite.

She hurried to the bus stop and waited for the bus that said "Downtown" and "International District." As she stepped up in the front door, she saw Alan and Jack get on in the rear. She hurried and sat down, acting as though she hadn't noticed. So, the two scared rabbits hadn't run very far at all. How odd that they were on the same bus going the same direction. Were they following her? And if so, why?

Perhaps she shouldn't get off at the Walgreen's after all. She'd get off a block sooner. But she'd never been downtown all by herself before. She didn't want to get lost.

While she was trying to figure out what to do, she saw Walgreen's Drugstore just down the street. And there were the Wakamutsu brothers standing outside waiting for her. If she were Margo Lane on the *Green Hornet,* she'd know something terribly clever to do to get Jack and Alan off her trail. But she was just plain old Audrey Harrington, and she had no idea what to do.

When the bus stopped in front of Walgreen's, she stood up and got off. Glancing back, she saw Alan and Jack getting off as well. They *were* following her.

She ran up to Kaneko and Abiko. Pushing the money into Abiko's hand, she grabbed the sack and blurted out, "Those two boys tried to beat up Frank. They followed me."

Just then, Alan yelled at them, "You Japs need to learn to stay in your own neighborhood."

"Quick," Kaneko said to his brother. "To the alley!"

They dashed between the buildings with Audrey on their

heels. Kaneko went to the left, Abiko to the right. Audrey jumped behind Kaneko. He was the bigger one.

She realized Jack and Alan weren't too smart when they both came running together right into the trap. Kaneko grabbed one and Abiko the other. The Wakamutsu boys were accomplished in jujitsu, having studied it for years. Before they knew what hit them, Jack and Alan were on their backs in the dirty alley.

"Come on, Audrey," Kaneko said, grabbing her arm. "Let's get you to the bus stop."

"Will they be all right?" she asked, looking back over her shoulder at the bewildered boys.

"We were gentle," Abiko assured her.

Stopping a moment, she called back to Jack and Alan, "My brother learned jujitsu from these boys. He'd have used it on you if he hadn't had a coughing attack."

Kaneko chuckled as he hurried her back out to Fifth Street. "That's not really true," he said. "We taught Frank only a few moves."

"Close enough," she said, glancing back to see if they were still following.

Abiko saw her looking. "Don't worry, Audrey. They won't want another helping of that treatment anytime soon."

The bus for Queen Anne Hill was pulling up. The boys took her right up to the door. Audrey noticed the bus driver frown as he looked at the two Japanese boys.

If he only knew, she thought as she found her seat. Waving good-bye to her friends, she sat back and finally breathed a big sigh of relief. Wait until she told Frank what happened.

When she got home, Frank was asleep. After he awoke later that evening, Mama made sure he drank a big cup of the herbal tea, which he said tasted "worse than terrible." Then

106

she insisted he go to bed early. That gave Audrey the opportunity to slip into his room and tell him the whole story.

He laughed as she described how Kaneko and Abiko jumped and kicked and chopped before Jack and Alan knew what hit them.

"I wish I could have seen it. Tell me again."

Mother had instructed Frank to lie down and stay still, but he was propped up in bed, soaking up Audrey's every word.

She described the scene all over again.

"I can't believe they'd follow you. Can they really hate the Japanese that much?"

"I don't know." Then she wondered, could the Golden Ring really hate her and Hulda as much as they did?

"There's one other thing I haven't told you yet," she said, grinning.

"What?"

"I told Jack and Alan that you knew jujitsu."

"You didn't." He smiled. "Did you really?"

"It wasn't really a lie. You know some, don't you?"

"Some," he agreed. He thought about that a minute. "I may go to the Wakamutsus' on Saturday. I could use a refresher. I never thought I'd need it before this." He took one of his pillows, fluffed it, and repositioned it. "I wouldn't ever want to hurt anyone, but maybe I could get the other boys' respect this way."

Audrey thought about that a minute. "I think we get respect by just being ourselves."

"I suppose so." Then Frank added, "I feel really bad that Kaneko and Abiko fought my battle for me. When the guys at school talk about how awful the Japanese are, I don't say one word in their defense." He shook his head. "That's just not right."

Audrey didn't know what to say to him. She knew how hard it was to take a stand when everyone was against you. "Pastor Colston said that Jesus could equip us to do the things we're supposed to do."

Frank nodded. "Yeah, I know. I heard him."

She didn't see how he could have heard when he was playing tic-tac-toe, but she didn't argue. "Well?"

"Well what?"

"How about if we pray together?" She could tell Frank was a little embarrassed. They'd often prayed as a family, but never just the two of them.

"You go ahead," he said.

"Bow your head," she told him. As they bowed their heads, she asked Jesus to equip both of them to do what He wanted them to do at school.

As she opened her eyes, she noticed how tired Frank looked. "You'd better get to sleep, or Mama will kill both of us."

He nodded in agreement. That proved how tired he was. And he was missing *Jack Armstrong, All American Boy* on the radio. That *really* proved how tired he was.

She tiptoed out and went to her room to study.

Much to her surprise, by the time Audrey had made perfect scores on the Wednesday spelling test three times in a row, no one said a word about it. She could hardly believe it. She still wasn't included, but at least no one was nagging at her all the time. And she loved her two afternoons a week with Miss LaVolette.

The sweet librarian was becoming a good friend. They discussed their favorite authors and told why they liked certain story plots better than others. Miss LaVolette even explained to Audrey what was required at college to become a librarian.

Audrey thought that would be the greatest job in the whole world.

Each week, Miss LaVolette trusted her with more and more responsibility. She surprised Audrey one afternoon by telling her she could be the story-reader in the first-grade classroom that afternoon. The first graders seemed to enjoy having Audrey in their classroom, but she was the one who had the most fun!

A week after the incident with Jack and Alan, Audrey and Frank were walking home from school together.

"You'll never guess what happened today," Frank said. He was smiling.

"Tell me."

"As usual the guys were going on and on again about how awful the Japanese were, and as simple as you please, I said, 'They're like any other group of people in the world. Some are good and some are bad.' "

"Frank. Did you really?"

"I sure did. Know what I said then?"

"What?"

"I said, 'Even Kato, the housekeeper on *Green Hornet,* is Japanese. And he's a good person.' "

"What did they say to that?"

"They said they guessed that was right. One of the guys pointed out that the Japanese who are attacking China are *awful* bad. I agreed with him, and then I said, 'But I bet not all the people who live in Japan agree with what they're doing—and not all the ones in Seattle agree, either.' "

"I'm so proud of you, Frank. Really proud of you."

"Thanks." He grinned at her.

"Did Jack or Alan say anything?"

He nodded. "Alan said that the Japanese invented the art

of jujitsu and that it was a swell form of self-defense."

Audrey laughed.

Then Frank said softly, "I'm sure glad you suggested we pray."

Chapter 14

In the Limelight

Spring seemed to woo Audrey outdoors, and she had to admit, Queen Anne Hill was a beautiful place. Much more beautiful than the International District. She loved to go roller skating near their house.

But getting off by herself was next to impossible these days. With Isabel taking on more baby-sitting jobs and Alice gone so much, Audrey became the catch-all girl. She was either keeping an eye on the twins or helping Mama cook, clean, and iron. Sometimes she raised a fuss and told Mama that Frank could watch the twins as well as she could. It seemed to her that Frank got off scot-free from everything.

Of course, that wasn't completely true because Dad made him wash the car, mow the lawn, and keep the garage clean. But that didn't take him very long at all.

On the Saturday afternoon before the quiz contest, Audrey asked permission to skate to Kinnear Park. It took a minute to get Mama's attention. The Mixmaster was whirring away as she mixed up a chocolate cake for supper. Mama turned it off and cleaned the beaters with a rubber spatula. Miraculously, the twins were nowhere in sight, so Mama handed Audrey a beater to lick.

As she cleaned off the last bit of chocolate batter, Audrey asked again if she could skate to the park.

"Kinnear Park?" Mama asked. "All by yourself?"

Audrey wanted to remind her that Frank went all over the neighborhood by himself on his bicycle, but she was afraid Mama would remind her that Frank was a boy and two years older.

"Yes, all by myself." She held up a science book. "I'd like to be able to study this before next Friday."

Mama raised her eyebrows. "Is the contest that close? My, how time flies." She wiped her hands on her apron and proceeded to grease the cake pans, lining them with waxed paper so the cake wouldn't stick. "It's Friday afternoon at two, right?"

Audrey nodded. She knew Mama planned to be there. "And I sure need to study."

"Yes, I suppose you do. I'm proud of you, Audrey. You've made such an improvement in your grades." She poured the batter into the pans, scraping out the last bit with the spatula. "I suppose you do need time alone." The bowl clinked as she set it down on the white enamel cabinet. "Oh, all right. But just for an hour. I suppose Frank can play with the twins for a while."

"Thank you, Mama." Audrey gave her mother a quick hug and ran to get her skates.

As she sat on the porch, tightening the skates on her shoes with her skate key, she said to the twins, "A cake bowl's sitting in on the counter waiting to be licked clean." While they ran inside, she grabbed her book and skated off as fast as she could.

It was a glorious day. The mist that had hung heavy that morning had lifted, and the sun beamed through the trees, making dappled patches in her path as she skated down the sidewalk toward the park.

She decided to go to the far side of the park, where she could find a spot that overlooked the sparkling waters of Elliott Bay. People were everywhere, walking, bicycling, skating, and pushing baby buggies. Cars stopped, and families lugged out their picnic baskets, looking around for vacant picnic tables.

Audrey sat on a park bench and took off her skates, made her way to a shade tree near a lily pond, and sat down to read the science book. In the distance, the bay spread out before her. Perfect! No sisters or brothers anywhere. Of course, that didn't include Steve. She would have loved to have had him come along. If he'd been there, he'd be reading a book as well.

As the afternoon sun moved across the sky, she'd get up periodically and move with the shade. Every once in a while, she'd glance up to look around at the people strolling by. At one point, a flash of red made her look off to her left. It was the unmistakable red cardigan belonging to Hulda Goddard and the unmistakable roll-step walk. Hulda walked up to the rock ledge that surrounded the pool and sat down. She sat there for a time, staring into the water.

Audrey wondered if the girl lived near the park. What a perfect opportunity it would be to talk and learn more about her. With no Golden Ring nearby to spoil things, maybe she could reach out and be a friend to Hulda.

Lifting her strapped-together skates over her shoulder and grabbing her book, Audrey stood up and walked toward the other girl. As she approached, she smiled and said, "Hello, Hulda."

The girl looked up at her, startled.

"I didn't mean to scare you. Do you come here often?" She turned and pointed back up the hill. "I live up that way about five or six blocks. That is, I think they're blocks. All the streets are so curvy in this neighborhood."

As she was talking along in her most friendly voice, Hulda stood up and simply walked off. Step-roll, step-roll, step-roll down the path toward the sidewalk.

Audrey stared after her. Such rudeness! Here she was trying her best to be nice, and the girl just walked away. Well, Hulda Goddard could just go on being lonely for all she cared. Audrey asked an elderly man sitting on a park bench what time it was and found out it was time to go home anyway.

Audrey had been in a spelling bee in third grade, so she knew a little bit about being asked questions in front of others. But the morning of the quiz contest, her stomach churned so she could hardly bear to watch Frank eating his Wheaties. She didn't even care that he got the brand new Jack Armstrong decoder badge out of the box.

Through the day, the tension grew until she felt she might burst wide open. She kept taking deep breaths, but that didn't help. Would she freeze when she stepped up on the stage?

Would her brain short-circuit because she was so tense? Answering Isabel's questions in the bedroom was much different than being on a stage with the whole school watching. Whatever possessed her to think she could do this? Only a few fourth graders even signed up. Most of the entrants were fifth and sixth graders. What chance did she have?

The twins were oblivious as they walked home for lunch, running along and laughing and acting silly. At the house, Audrey told her mother she couldn't eat a bite, but Mama insisted she at least eat an apple. "It's light," she said. "And you need something in your stomach."

Audrey forced down the apple, reading a history book as she ate, then hurried back to school. The contest was to begin at two o'clock. The hands on the classroom pendulum clock barely moved for an entire hour.

When Mrs. Brumley said it was time for those who had entered the contest to be dismissed to go to the auditorium, Audrey wasn't sure her legs would carry her. She felt weak all over. Perhaps she would faint dead away, and then she wouldn't have to worry about the contest at all.

Four long rows of chairs were arranged on the stage for the participants. Audrey glanced around at the others, but no one appeared to be as nervous as she was. She sat down and folded her damp, clammy hands in her lap. Then, reaching in her pocket, she pulled out her flowered handkerchief and began to twist the corner of it. That gave her hands something to do.

Mama and the twins slipped in the rear door and took seats near the back of the room. Barb give a shy little wave. Students began filing in, and Audrey saw Frank come in and take his seat. She knew he was rooting for her.

Within a few minutes, the entire auditorium was packed, and the principal stepped to the lectern to give the welcome address. He explained the rules, saying that each student, when asked a question, must stand to answer. If he or she failed to answer correctly in the designated time, that person must leave the stage and take a seat down front.

"The teacher asking the questions will indicate the category," he continued, "whether arithmetic, science, history, or language. We've attempted to include an equal mix. This contest is for the versatile student. The well-read student."

As he said that, Audrey happened to catch Miss LaVolette's eye. The librarian smiled at her. That smile bolstered Audrey's courage.

Then the questions began. Mr. Curtiss, the sixth grade teacher, called out, "Audrey Harrington." She jumped to her feet. Her chair scooted and made a clattering noise on the floor. There were a few snickers. She felt her face flush.

"The category is language," he said, paying no attention to her clumsiness. "In this sentence, 'Johnny climbed up the hill,' what part of speech is the word *climbed*?"

Audrey swallowed hard. How she wished she could have a glass of water. "The word *climbed* is a verb."

"Correct," said Mr. Curtiss. "You may be seated."

As she sat down, she released a deep sigh. She'd done it. She'd actually answered the first question, and she was still in.

Three of the students were out on the very first round.

On the second round, her question was history. Mr. Curtiss cleared his throat. "Give the date when Fort Sumter fell into Confederate hands," he said. Then added, "Give the day, month, and year."

Audrey closed her eyes and forced herself to breathe deeply. "April," she said. "April 12, 1861."

"Correct," Mr. Curtiss said, smiling, and Audrey sat back down.

Her biggest fear was a word problem in math. For some reason, figures didn't compute as quickly in her head as facts.

A sixth grade boy named Darren Lockhart, who, according to Frank, was one of the smartest boys in his class, moved over beside her as empty chairs were taken from the stage. As he did, he looked over at her and smiled. He didn't seem a bit nervous. They were competing against one another, and yet he smiled at her. His smile seemed to say, "Enjoy yourself. This is fun."

She smiled back at him. As she did, strangely enough, the agonizing tightness in her chest eased up. Between questions she'd been staring hard at the floor in front of her feet. Now she allowed herself to look out over the crowd. Suddenly it occurred to her that there was nothing to be nervous about. Or to be afraid of. So what if she got a word problem and it was hard? So what if she missed it? She'd come this far, and there would always be next year. She was up there doing her very best, and that was all that mattered.

There were seven students left on the stage when she received her first word problem. "If three girls each had a basket containing a dozen oranges, and they wanted to give nine friends an equal number of oranges, how many oranges would each friend receive?"

Audrey began to figure in her head. She had only a few minutes. Three dozen oranges would be thirty-six, divided by nine. "Each friend would receive four oranges," she said.

"Correct," said Mr. Curtiss.

When she sat down, she heard Darren whisper, "Good job, fourth grader."

By now her nervousness had transformed into exhilaration. She truly was having fun! So when she and Darren were the only students left on the stage, it was as though the two of them shared a private joke.

"Darren Lockhart."

Darren stood to his feet.

"The category is history. Give the date when King John sealed the Magna Carta at Runnymede."

"King John sealed the Magna Carta on June 15, 1225."

"That is *not* correct," Mr. Curtiss said.

Darren sat down. And he was still smiling. Audrey wondered if maybe he already had a set of encyclopedias at his house. According to the rules, if she missed the question as well, he would be given yet another question, and the contest would continue.

As her name was called, she stood. The question was repeated. But she knew. The year wasn't 1225. It was 1215.

As soon as she gave the correct answer and Mr. Curtiss said, "Correct," the entire auditorium burst into loud applause. Darren was shaking her hand and congratulating her, telling her what a good job she'd done. Mr. Curtiss patted her back. Miss LaVolette was hugging her. Frank came up on stage to tell her how proud he was of her. Mother was there, and the twins were bouncing around her like two little jack-in-the-boxes.

"Audrey won! Audrey won!" they chanted. And Mama didn't tell them to hush.

Even old Mrs. Brumley was on the stage fussing over her.

When everything had calmed down, Mr. Curtiss announced that the set of encyclopedias would be delivered to the Harrington home the following week. Then he said, "This is the first time in the history of the quiz contest that a fourth grader has won."

Applause echoed through the auditorium. Audrey couldn't remember ever being so happy.

Since it was time for school to be dismissed, the building emptied rather quickly. Mama and the twins waited in the front hall while Audrey went to her classroom to get her books and jacket. When she came out of the room, Marie Sikes was standing in the hall almost as though she were waiting for Audrey.

Audrey started to walk right past her. After all, no one in the Golden Ring had ever spoken to her except to torment her.

But Marie said, "Audrey?"

Audrey stopped and looked at her.

"I just wanted to tell you I think you did a swell job. I would have been scared spitless up there." The girl gave a weak smile.

"Thank you, Marie. It's nice of you to say so. I was pretty scared at first."

"I just wanted you to know. . ." She stopped a minute. "I'm glad you didn't let what the girls. . ." Catching herself, she began again. "I'm glad you didn't let what *we* said stop you."

She left without another word.

CHAPTER 15

Summertime

Every time Audrey walked through their living room and saw the beautiful encyclopedia set with its embossed burgundy covers, she wanted to burst with pride. She told everyone in the family that they were welcome to use the books at any time. "Just make sure you put them back where they belong, and don't handle them with dirty hands," she said.

The evening after the contest, Mama let them all stay up until Dad arrived home. They were all in the kitchen when he arrived, and together they had a celebration in Audrey's honor. Dad looked tired, but she could tell he was very happy.

"Audrey, I don't know what happened to cause you to care about your studies again," he said, "but whatever it was, I'm so grateful."

After that, the school year was a breeze. Other kids began to talk to her. Even Darren smiled and said hello when they passed in the hallways and saw one another out on the playground. While Grace wasn't at all polite, she stopped attacking Audrey.

Now if someone called her Audrey Einstein, it didn't sound like an insult. It sounded like a compliment, and they smiled when they said it.

Each evening, Mama listened closely to Edward R. Murrow's news reports. As a European correspondent, Murrow gave the news right on the spot. The news in May was not good. All of Holland had been overrun by the Nazis in four short days. Belgium was taken almost as quickly.

"Like little dominoes," Mama said. She kept her chair close to the big console radio in the living room and listened as she knitted blankets and clothing for those in need who were in the midst of war.

School came to an end, and the wonderful, happy, carefree days of summer arrived. Frank built a wagon for the twins. He tied it to his bicycle, and with Audrey on her skates, the four of them traveled throughout the neighborhood. Frank spent hours in the backyard practicing the new jujitsu moves that Kaneko and Abiko had taught him. In turn, he tried to teach them to Eddie.

Mama let them go to the drugstore for candy and double-dip ice cream cones, which dripped sticky drops on them all the way home. And Saturday movie matinees became part of every week.

That first Saturday in June, they went to see a Gene Autry

western. The twins liked Gene Autry. Audrey's favorite western star was Roy Rogers. Frank liked Tom Mix because Tom just "chased the bad guys and didn't stop to sing songs."

But first there was the *Movietone* newsreel, and that's where they learned about the evacuation from Dunkirk, France. The film showed British soldiers who had been trying to keep Germany from invading France running away from Hitler's army. The British government sent anything that could float across the English Channel to bring their soldiers home. Audrey watched ordinary citizens risk their lives to get destroyers, tugs, cross-channel packets, paddlewheel ferries, fishing boats, yachts, and dinghies across the water. Many made the trip again and again.

"When the evacuation was over," said the booming voice, "more than three hundred thousand men had been carried to safety. While it was a triumph of undaunting human spirit, it is at the same time a military disaster."

Audrey knew from what she'd heard Mama and Dad saying that France now stood totally alone in Europe. Could they hold Hitler at bay? The world would find out soon enough.

A couple weeks later, Audrey came into the living room to see her mother weeping. "Mama," she said, hurrying over to her chair. "What is it? It's not Jim, is it?"

Mama dabbed at her cheeks with a handkerchief and shook her head. "France stood so strong through the Great War. She sacrificed so many of her sons. And now she's fallen. It's a sad day in history, Audrey. A very sad day for a glorious people."

Audrey didn't know what to make of it all. Even Italy, whom most Americans felt would side with the Allies, had declared war on both Britain and France earlier in the month. Was there a country in the world that wasn't at war?

And then there was the election coming that fall. Dad and Mama and Steve and Alice discussed it at length whenever the four of them were together—usually on Saturday nights and Sunday afternoons. No one knew for sure what President Roosevelt's plans were. Would he run for office for a third term? No president in history had ever served for three full terms. It was unheard of.

"I'm sure he must be weary," Mama said, her knitting needles clicking in rhythm. A fan by the window was moving the warm, humid air around the living room.

"Yes," Dad agreed. "But changing horses in the middle of the stream could be disastrous. We desperately need his leadership now."

Audrey and Barb were lying on the living room floor as Audrey helped Barb cut out her new Shirley Temple paper dolls from the paper doll book. Barb had already accidentally cut off the pant leg of one of the cute ski outfits, so she'd asked Audrey to help. At Dad's words, Barb looked up.

"Where's the horse, Dad?" she asked.

"It's just a figure of speech, Barb," Audrey explained. "There's not really any horse."

"Good leadership is always necessary for a country like ours," Dad went on, "but at a time like this, it's vital. We need Roosevelt just like Britain needs Churchill."

At the next Saturday matinee, Audrey saw film clips of Hitler standing outside the railway carriage where he'd forced France's officials to surrender. More than a million French, the narrator said, had been taken as prisoners. Audrey couldn't picture a million people—especially not as prisoners. It was just too awful to comprehend.

"We helped the French in the last war," Frank said that evening at supper, "why don't we help them now?"

Audrey wondered the same thing. Couldn't someone do something to help?

Mama shook her head. "It's not that simple, I'm afraid."

"You see, Frank," Steve spoke up, "war is a terrible thing. It costs a great deal of money, and more than that, it costs lives. Many Americans feel that the war in Europe is none of our business. They think we should stay out of it."

"But will Hitler allow us to keep minding our own business?" Frank asked.

"That, my dear brother," Steve said, slapping Frank on the shoulder, "is a very, very good question. One I hope Congress will soon address."

Dad and Mama both seemed to breathe a little easier when they learned that Roosevelt had agreed to run again. At the Democratic convention in July, he was nominated on the very first ballot. And because her parents were pleased, Audrey was pleased as well.

Several times during the summer, when Audrey was able to slip away to Kinnear Park to be alone and read, she'd see Hulda. But she made no attempt to be friendly to the girl. She didn't even wave. Hulda sometimes glanced in her direction. Audrey would look at her, then look back at her book and keep on reading. If Hulda didn't want to be friends, there was nothing Audrey could do about it.

One afternoon as Audrey was strapping her skates on, a voice from behind her said, "You dropped this."

Hulda was holding out the special bookmark that Miss LaVolette had given Audrey. It was a gift for having won the quiz contest.

"Thank you, Hulda. I wouldn't have wanted to lose that. It's special to me."

Hulda nodded. "I thought so. Miss LaVolette likes you a lot."

Audrey didn't know what to say to that. She put the bookmark in her library book and strapped on her other skate. Just then it occurred to her that Hulda would never be able to skate. It was a sad thought. No one probably had any idea how much this girl suffered because she was lame.

Audrey determined to try once again to be nice. But when she looked up, Hulda was gone. Shaking her head, she wondered if it had been this hard for King David to get to know Miphibosheth.

CHAPTER 16

Hulda's Visit

When Audrey opened her eyes, it was still dark. What had awakened her? she wondered. She punched at her pillow, turned over, and tried to go back to sleep. There it was again. Whimpering. Audrey sat up in bed and looked over at Barb. Her little sister was kicking and whimpering in her sleep.

Audrey slipped out of bed and stepped over to her sister's bed. "Barb," she said softly. Then she lay her hand on her sister's shoulder. "Barb, honey, what's the matter? Are you having a dream?"

Barb roused a little. "A bad dream," she said.

"Here's your Shirley Temple doll." Audrey picked up the doll from the floor and put it in Barb's waiting arms.

Barb mumbled her thanks and went back to sleep.

The bad dreams came several times over the next few nights. Finally Audrey felt she should tell Mama about it.

"It's those movies you children have been seeing," was Mama's explanation. "I probably shouldn't let the little ones go with you."

Audrey had to admit the newsreels had been pretty scary lately. But when Mama said something about the twins not going to the movies every Saturday, they pitched such a fit, she decided to relent.

Audrey talked with Barb, trying to find out if something was bothering her, but Barb just shrugged her little shoulders and said everything was all right. Audrey wished she knew how to help her little sister stop having nightmares.

One afternoon when Frank was in the backyard practicing jujitsu with Eddie, Audrey asked Barb if she'd like to walk to the park, just the two of them. Barb's eyes lit up.

"I sure would," she said

After getting Mama's permission, they were on their way. Barb held tightly to Audrey's hand as they walked up one hill and down another until they reached Kinnear Park. Audrey took her sister to the playground, where they played on the slippery slide and swings until they were hot and sweaty.

They bought cones of sweetened shaved ice from the sidewalk vendor and took them to the lily pond. There they ate the refreshing treat and watched the shiny goldfish. The paper cones got all soggy before they were half finished with them. Barb's had a little leak in the bottom, trailing red drips down the front of her playsuit. After Barb drank the very last drops,

Audrey took the cups to the trash can. When she came back to where Barb was sitting, Hulda was looking at them.

"You don't have a book," she said to Audrey.

It was like a statement and a question all mixed together. "No, I don't. I came to play with Barb." Motioning to Barb, she said, "This is my little sister, Barbara. We call her Barb."

Hulda nodded. "I saw you walk her home from school every day at lunch."

"Oh yeah. I guess you did." Turning to Barb, she said, "Barbara, this is one of my classmates. Her name is Hulda Goddard."

Barb looked up and said, "Hi, Hulda. Sit down with us. Want to?"

And she did.

It was a rather awkward time. Making conversation with Hulda was not an easy job, but at least Audrey learned more than she'd ever known before.

"My grandpa was here before any of these fancy people," Hulda said, waving her hand in the air as though to take in all of Queen Anne Hill. "He says we were first. We were first."

Audrey wasn't sure what to say, but Barb piped up and said, "We just came last year. So we're sort of new."

"I'm not new here," Hulda said. "I've lived here ever since I was born."

"Do you live with your grandfather?" Audrey asked.

Hulda nodded. "I live with Grandpa."

"Where are your parents?"

"Dead," she said. And that was that. She got up to leave.

"Come by to see us at our house sometime," Barb said.

"Yes, Hulda," Audrey added. "Come for a visit." She called out the address, but Hulda walked away without looking back.

An orphan. Hulda was as alone as Little Orphan Annie in

the funny papers. Only she didn't have any Daddy Warbucks. Or even a nice dog named Sandy.

"Thank you for taking me to the park," Barb said to Audrey as they walked back home. "I like being with you."

"You're welcome, Barb."

Later, Audrey thought about what Barb had said. It sounded like something she would have said to Steve or Alice. She loved to be with them and have them pay attention to her. But both of them were so busy. Alice was hardly ever at home anymore. And Steve was either working or studying. It never occurred to Audrey that Barb might feel left out as well. Had her little sister needed her when she had her nose stuck in a book all the time? Or when she finagled for ways to get off by herself?

Perhaps being with Barb wasn't like being the baby of the family after all. Perhaps it was time for Audrey to take her place in the family as Barb's older sister.

The next time Barb had a nightmare, she mumbled words instead of just kicking the covers. Audrey hurried over to see if she could make any sense of the mumbling. She sat on the edge of Barb's bed and leaned her head down close. The words sounded like, "I don't know. I don't know how. It's too hard." Then she started whimpering.

"What's too hard, Barb? Tell Audrey. What's too hard?"

In the dim glow of the night-light, she saw Barb's eyes flutter open. Then she sat up and threw her arms around Audrey's neck, clinging to her so tightly, Audrey thought she was going to be choked. "I don't wanna go," she wailed pitifully.

"Wait, wait a minute." With Barb still clinging to her neck, Audrey lifted her little sister so she could reach the lamp on the bedside table. "Wake up, Barb. Tell me what you were dreaming about."

Barb let go of Audrey's neck and rubbed her eyes with her fists. She looked up at Audrey. "I had a dream."

"I know. A bad dream. Now tell me what it was about."

Snuggling close to Audrey, she said, "Don't make me have to go to first grade, Audrey. I'm scared."

Audrey buried her face in Barb's soft curls. "Now, how can a big girl like you be scared of school?" she asked. "That's the strangest thing I've ever heard of." She leaned back and look at Barb's worry-filled little face. "You've already been in school for a whole year. Why are you afraid now?"

Audrey remembered a year ago when Barb was dancing all over the room in her excitement to go to kindergarten. It was Audrey who was afraid and dreaded going.

"That was kindergarten," Barb said. She reached over and pulled Shirley Temple onto her lap. "All we do in kindergarten is play. First grade is real hard. I don't even know how to read."

Audrey shook her head. So that was what was causing the bad dreams. "Who told you first grade was so hard?"

"Mabel."

"And who is Mabel?"

"A girl in my kindergarten class."

Audrey put her arm around Barb and pulled her close. "If Mabel was in kindergarten with you, how does she know about first grade?"

Barb shrugged. "I dunno."

"She doesn't know. But I do, because I've been in first grade. And I can tell you that you will do fine."

"Are you sure?"

"Sure I'm sure. Would I lie to my favorite little sister?"

Barb laughed. "I'm your *only* little sister."

"Tell you what. Tomorrow you and I will get a story book,

and I'll show you some words and tell you what the letters are. Would you like that?"

"You hear that, Shirley Temple?" Barb said to the doll in her lap. "Audrey's gonna help me learn to read."

"Now you lie down and go back to sleep." Audrey leaned down and kissed her sister's sweet face. "Everything's going to be all right. G'night, honey."

"Night, Audrey."

"Our Gal Sunday," the radio announcer said, "the story of an orphan girl named Sunday from the little mining town of Silver Creek, Colorado. . . ."

Mama turned the radio up a little. Audrey knew this was one of her favorite shows. Audrey was putting the iron and ironing board away. The twins had had their lunch, and Mama had put them down for a nap. Audrey was glad the ironing was finished. It was too hot to iron. Steve was asleep on the couch. He'd had a wisdom tooth extracted that morning, so his boss told him to stay home. Mama had tried her best to keep everyone quiet so he could rest.

"The story that asks the question," the announcer of *Our Gal Sunday* went on, "can this girl from a mining town in the West find happiness as the wife of a wealthy and titled Englishman, Lord Henry Brinthrope?"

Audrey knew there was never going to be an answer to that question. If the question were answered, the show would be over.

Just then, a knock sounded at the front door. Audrey hurried to answer it before the noise woke Steve. To her surprise, Hulda stood at the door. "I came to visit," the girl said in her raspy voice. "Like you said."

CHAPTER 17

New Friends

Audrey stood at the door dumbfounded. What was she supposed to say? Or do? Hulda evidently had no idea it was not polite to drop in for a visit without phoning first.

"Hello, Hulda. Won't you come in? It's good to see you."

She led Hulda into the kitchen. "Mother," she said, "this is Hulda Goddard. From school."

"Welcome, Hulda. I remember seeing you at school." Audrey could tell by the look on Mama's face that she was thinking back. "At the Christmas program, I believe it was."

Audrey winced. Why did her mother have to mention the

Christmas program, of all things? But to her surprise, Hulda smiled. Audrey hadn't seen the girl smile very often.

"The program," she said, "when I fell down."

"Oh, yes." Mother laughed. "Yes. That's right. I believe both of you took a tumble that night." She folded a damp dish towel and hung it over the rods above the sink. "The twins are napping in my bedroom, Audrey. Why don't you take Hulda to your room?"

Audrey wasn't sure what she was going to do once they got to her room. Never had she felt so awkward. She led the way upstairs and down the hallway toward her room. "My older sisters' room is here," she said, waving a hand in that direction. "And Barb and I are right in here."

"Pretty," Hulda said as she stepped inside. "Your room is pretty." She looked around. "Do you have your own radio?"

Audrey shook her head. "Only Steve has his own. His room is down at the end. Sometimes if there's something real special on, I can ask permission to take the one from the kitchen and bring it up here."

Hulda nodded but said nothing. She walked over to the dressing table and sat down, looking at the items there. She picked up a couple bobby pins out of the plastic dish where Audrey kept them.

Glancing at Hulda's hair, which was never fixed properly, Audrey said, "Want me to show you how to put your hair up in pin curls?"

Hulda jumped up from the tufted stool and walked to the door. "You want to make me different?" she said. She strode out into the hallway, and Audrey hurried after her, bewildered. "That's what Grace Farmington would do. Change me. Make me different."

As Audrey followed her down the stairs, she realized she

had a lot to learn about Hulda Goddard. And it was going to take a lot of time.

At the bottom of the stairs, Hulda suddenly stopped. "Where are the encyclopedias?"

Forgetting that Steve was resting, Audrey pointed to the living room. "In there."

Without asking, Hulda walked in the room and looked at the books sitting on the shelf. Steve opened one eye to see what the disturbance was, readjusted the ice pack on his face, and said nothing.

Audrey stepped up beside Hulda. "If it hadn't been for you, I would never have won these."

"I know," the girl replied.

"Thank you for saying what you did that day in the library."

"It was the truth," Hulda answered. She turned back to the hallway and headed in her roll-step gait to the front door.

Not waiting for Audrey to open the door, she let herself out. Going down the sidewalk, Hulda called, "I'll come back again."

That evening at supper, Mama told the story about Hulda coming to visit, unannounced. Audrey could tell by Mama's tone that she hadn't minded one bit. "That girl may be a little slow in speech and in her ways," Mama said, "but she's certainly not dumb."

Audrey thought that was a good description. "God loves her just like King David loved Miphibosheth."

"Who?" Frank asked, laying down the pork chop he'd been devouring. "Who in the world is Miphibo. . . Whatever you said."

"If you'd listen in church, you'd know." She explained

about Miphibosheth and how King David hunted for him throughout the land, then gave him a place at the king's table.

Steve, who was eating a clear soup instead of pork chops, said, "Hey, little sis. I'm proud of you." Putting down his spoon, he got up from his place to come over and give her a hug.

"But I didn't do anything," she said.

"I saw you with Hulda," he said. "How kind you were with her. So in a way you're right—it really isn't what you *do*, it's who you *are*. And you are one sweet girl." Before sitting back down, he gave her another hug.

Audrey basked in his praise. It made her feel all grown up. She'd gained something that was far better than a piggyback ride—she'd gained her older brother's respect.

Each evening out on the porch swing, Audrey read to Barb from *The Bobbsey Twins in the Country*. Barb especially liked the book because there were two sets of twins in the family. Freddie and Flossie were the two younger ones, and Nan and Bert were the two older ones.

Audrey read slowly and pointed out words and named letters. By the time they were finished with the book, Barb was saying, "T-w-i-n-s. That spells twins. I can read *and* spell both." Of course, she couldn't really read. Not yet anyway. But that wasn't important. What mattered was that the nightmares had ceased. Audrey never realized before how little it took to make her little sister happy.

Money wasn't as tight as it had been the previous school year, so Audrey had three new dresses with which to begin school. And a few new skirts and blouses as well. And, of course, her dungarees.

Frank would be going to junior high and would no longer be walking to school with her each day. She'd miss that. But she knew she'd be all right this year.

Before the first day, she told Mama she'd need lunch money.

Mama's eyebrows went up. "Oh really? You're not coming home for lunch this year?"

Audrey shook her head. "The twins will be at school all day, so there's no need for me to walk home. I may just as well stay there, too."

Mama nodded. "My goodness. All of my children in school all day. I won't know what to do with myself."

Audrey didn't believe that for a minute.

When Audrey walked into the fifth grade classroom, she looked around at the familiar faces and felt right at home. Mrs. Peterson, their teacher, was a bright-eyed lady whom Audrey knew would be much more on top of things than Mrs. Brumley ever was. Mrs. Brumley, she soon learned, had retired and would not be back. That was good news for this year's fourth graders.

Grace Farmington was in the center of her friends, the same as always. She was bronzed with a summer tan, and her honey-hair was more golden than ever. Someone said she'd spent the summer traveling with her parents.

And, of course, Hulda appeared wearing her frayed red cardigan. She actually smiled at Audrey when she walked in the door. Amazing.

When the day got underway, Mrs. Peterson made various announcements. One important announcement was that Miss Browne had joined the Red Cross. "So," Mrs. Peterson added, "since the school has been unable to hire a new physical education instructor, we'll have regular recess this year."

The class broke into a spontaneous cheer.

Mrs. Peterson put her finger over her mouth. "Shh. No talking aloud without raising our hand first."

It was going to be a very good year.

As soon as Audrey could do so, she hurried to the library to see Miss LaVolette. She had some unfinished business about a lie she had told. Now she could tell the truth about the torn book, and it would no longer be like tattling. Miss LaVolette gave her a hug and said she forgave her for the lie, and Audrey felt a load go off her shoulders. She'd carried that weight around for much too long.

School had been in session only a few days when the terrible news broke of Germany bombing London. Nearly a thousand bombers struck at the heart of the great city. No one could believe it. Killing innocent civilians on purpose—that was unheard of.

"This, if anything," Audrey's father said, "will raise the sympathies of the people of the United States for the Brits."

On the newsreels, Audrey saw young schoolchildren hiding in trenches while the battle raged overhead. She saw the British loading their children onto trains to send them into the countryside to live with other families until the Blitz, as the bombing was called, was over.

The terrifying Battle of Britain dragged on through the autumn. Many people, including her teacher, Mrs. Peterson, said they didn't see how Britain could hold on much longer. But the Brits *did* hold on. And their prime minister, Winston Churchill, said it was England's "finest hour."

"It's the Royal Air Force," Dad kept saying with a distinct note of pride in his voice. "I've always said, it's the airplanes that will win this war. We need to be making more of them."

Audrey wasn't exactly sure what Dad did every day, working long hours at the Boeing plant, but she was confident he had a part in helping Britain shoot down the German planes and protect and defend their homeland. And she was immensely proud of him.

Some days Hulda sat with her during lunch. Some days she didn't. That's the way Hulda was. Audrey was trying to learn to appreciate her new friend's ups and downs—and not to try to change her. Though Audrey was nothing like King David, she still felt as though she were allowing Miphibosheth the privilege of sitting at the table. Perhaps someday she'd be able to tell Hulda about how much Jesus, the real King, loved her.

Two girls in fifth grade came over to Audrey's table one day at lunch and asked if they could sit with her. "Sure," she answered and scooted over to make room.

One of the two girls, Merilee, was new. Her father had moved to Seattle to work at Boeing, so they had something in common. The other girl, Sally, had been there last year.

As they sat down, Sally began to tell Merilee all about the quiz contest and how Audrey had won first place, just as though it had happened the day before. Audrey blushed, but it made her feel good that Sally seemed to enjoy talking about it. She sounded as though she were proud to know Audrey.

From then on, the three spent time together at recess and during the lunch hour. And neither Merilee nor Sally seemed to mind at all when Hulda sat with them at lunch.

One day as they were eating together and joking about the lukewarm spaghetti, Audrey looked up to see Marie Sikes standing by the table. Marie looked as though she wanted to say something. Hulda was sitting by Audrey's side, with Merilee and Sally opposite them.

"Hello, Marie," Audrey said. "Want to sit down? There's room."

"Thanks, but I can't." She nodded over toward the Golden

Ring, sitting in another part of the cafeteria. "The others are expecting me to sit with them."

Audrey looked at her and waited a minute. "Did you need something?" she asked.

"I wanted to ask you a favor," she said. Her voice was soft, as though she didn't want anyone to hear. "Audrey, do you think you could help me with my long division? I'm having a terrible time understanding it."

Before Audrey could answer, Hulda spoke up. "Well, naturally she can help. Don't you remember who won the encyclopedia set last spring?"

To Audrey's surprise, Marie smiled. "I know she *can*, Hulda. I'm asking if she *will*."

Hulda chuckled. "She'll do that, too!"

Audrey nodded. "Hulda's right. How about if we work on it tomorrow during library hour?"

"Swell. Thanks. See you then."

As Marie walked away, Audrey wondered if that was the first time Marie had ever talked to Hulda in a civil tone.

Just then, Hulda leaned over and said, "Don't look now, but the Golden Ring is getting a little tarnished."

The four girls burst into laughter.

CHAPTER 18

A Leader for the Future

The Wakamutsus' small living room was jam-packed with Harringtons, crowded around the radio with their hosts to listen to the election returns.

Dad had been let off work early so he could vote.

When he'd gotten home, he'd told Mama, "Call the Wakamutsus. See if they want company this evening. We'll all listen to the returns together."

The Wakamutsus were happy for their friends to drop by. Now they sat around eating, talking, and waiting for the news.

Just a week before the election, President Roosevelt had

ordered the first peacetime military draft in the history of the United States. All eligible young men had signed up and been assigned numbers from 1 to 7,836. On the newsreel at the movies, Audrey saw Secretary of War Henry L. Stimson draw a number from the goldfish bowl that had been used during the Great War. He handed the number to President Roosevelt, and the president read out, "One hundred fifty-eight." All young men who had been assigned that number were now destined for boot camp.

Audrey looked over at Steve's young, handsome face smiling at some joke that Mr. Wakamutsu had made, and she wondered if he would be marching off to war one day. She looked over at Alice, who seemed to have turned from a girl to a grown-up woman overnight as she worried about Jim's safety in the Philippines.

It was nearly midnight, and the twins were asleep—Barb on Dad's lap, and Eddie in a corner on the floor. Yoshiko and Isabel were in Yoshiko's bedroom listening to phonograph records.

Suddenly the news broke. Republican nominee Wendell Wilkie had conceded defeat. The entire room broke into a rousing cheer. Even quiet, demure Mrs. Wakamutsu was cheering. They were waving their cups of tea and bottles of Coca-Cola in a rousing salute.

"Wait a minute," Steve said, waving his hand. "Wilkie's about to speak."

They instantly became quiet so they could listen to Mr. Wilkie's words.

"No matter which side you were on," came the defeated candidate's voice over the airwaves, "this great expression of faith in the free system of government must have given hope wherever man hopes to be free."

Then, referring to Mr. Roosevelt, Mr. Wilkie said, "He is your president. He is my president. And we will pray God may guide his hand during the next four years."

Mr. Wakamutsu reached over and turned down the volume. "He is right. We must pray."

He bowed his head, and the others did the same. As Audrey listened to the prayer of this gentle, kind Japanese-American man, she, too, prayed for their president. And she prayed that God would equip him with the wisdom to guide their country through these perilous times.

There's More!

The American Adventure continues with *War Strikes*. Frank and Audrey Harrington's lives are turned upside down when Japan attacks Pearl Harbor. Suddenly the United States is at war. Blackouts, victory gardens, and rationing become part of everyday life.

Their oldest brother, Steve, announces that he's enlisted in the army. Then the government announces that all Japanese-Americans must leave their homes and go to huge internment camps. This means the Wakamutsus must leave Seattle.

What will happen to the Wakamutsus and the Fairfax? Will Steve be all right or will he get wounded or even die? And how can Frank and Audrey help their sister, Alice, when she learns that her fiancé is missing in action?

You're in for the ultimate
American Adventure!
Collect all 48 books!